I0578377

A DARK DRABBLES ANTHOLOGY

Compiled & Edited by D Kershaw

Also available from Black Hare Press

DARK DRABBLE ANTHOLOGIES

WORLDS
ANGELS
MONSTERS
BEYOND
UNRAVEL
APOCALYPSE
LOVE
HATE
OCEANS
ANCIENTS

Twitter: @BlackHarePress
Facebook: BlackHarePress
Website: www.BlackHarePress.com

Love, A Dark Drabbles Anthology title is
Copyright © 2020 Black Hare Press
First published in Australia in March 2020 by Black Hare Press

The authors of the individual stories retain the copyright of the works featured in this anthology.

All characters and events in this publication, other than those clearly in the public domain, are fictitious and any resemblance to real persons, living or dead, is purely coincidental.

All rights reserved. No part of this production may be reproduced, stored in a retrieval system, or transmitted, in any form or by any means, electronic, mechanical, photocopying, recording or otherwise, without the prior permission of the publisher and copyright owner.

Paperback : ISBN 978-1-925809-53-4
Hardcover : ISBN 978-1-925809-54-1

Cover Design by Dawn Burdett
Book Formatting by Ben Thomas

Why I love thee?;

Ask why the seawind wanders,;

Why the shore is aflush with the tide,;

Why the moon through heaven meanders;

Like seafaring ships that ride;

On a sullen, motionless deep;;

Why the seabirds are fluttering the strand;

Where the waves sing themselves to sleep;

And starshine lives in the curves of the sand!;

Carl Sadakichi Hartmann, *Why I Love Thee?* **1904**

Table of Contents

Foreword

Have you ever been so obsessed with someone that thoughts of them envelop everything in your life, fill your every waking moment with desire, permeate your dreams…make you crazier than a box of frogs?

Have you ever been so devout in your love for another that all rational thought goes out the window and you'd do everything in your power to keep them close, no matter what? Maybe keep them locked away…? Kill for them…?

Kill them…?

We found one hundred and fifty authors who have been there, just like you, and these are their twisted tales of dark devotion.

Love and kisses
D. Kershaw & Ben Thomas
Black Hare Press

She Loves Me
by Kathy Slater Neilsen

PLUCK. "She loves me." He coos with a sickly grin.

PLUCK. "She loves me not." His smile fades, and he fidgets with displeasure.

PLUCK. "She loves me." He shudders with glee.

PLUCK. "She loves me not." His wail pierces the stillness.

She stirs beneath him, barely conscience.

PLUCK. "She loves me." His maniacal laughter pulls her from her dark escape. The pain is excruciating yet she hasn't the strength to scream

PLUCK. "She loves me not." He looks down at a small pile of fingers and toes. They lie in an expanding pool of her blood.

PLUCK. "She loves me."

Kathy Slater Neilsen has always possessed a passion for writing as well as reading. Her early writing career included freelance non-fiction. Then, as is often the case, life lead her on a different journey that included motherhood and a small business. But she never stopped writing. Now retired and living on the east coast she is currently writing fiction and is focused on short stories and flash fiction.

Pen is Mightier Than the Scalpel?
by Steven Holding

For her to see exactly what she means to me, a clear demonstration of my devotion is required.

One magnificent gesture requested; that all I possess, each fibre of my being, is eagerly surrendered in her honour.

I readily accept such a test.

At dawn, I arrive at her doorstep, razor-sharp blade clutched to my chest. Like a master artist, the silky steel separates until scarlet stains skin.

The offer of an ear is met with disdain.

I happily slice once again.

Another earlobe. A nose. It's not enough.

I continue to cut until each tiny piece has come off.

Steven Holding lives with his family in the United Kingdom. His stories have appeared both online and in print. Most recently his work has featured in the collections 'TREMBLING WITH FEAR YEAR TWO', 'SPLASH OF INK', and the anthologies 'MONSTERS', 'BEYOND' and 'DARK MOMENTS - YEAR ONE' from Black Hare Press. He is currently working upon further short fiction and a novel. Website: www.stevenholding.co.uk

God is Love
by Amber M. Simpson

The fire raged, burning bright. Thick black clouds of smoke billowed into the sky, blotting out the sun. Wood splintered and cracked as the building's structure broke down like common kindling.

Though the screams inside died out long ago, Father Lyle remained outside the church, fervent prayers falling from his lips.

God told him what he wanted; it was his job to see it through.

His heart swelled with joyous love as he watched the fire he'd created for the Almighty Father, sending home so many blessed souls.

"God is love!" he cried, stepping into the flames to join them.

Amber M. Simpson is a dark fiction writer from Northern Kentucky with a penchant for horror and fantasy. Her work has been published in multiple anthologies, as well as online. She assists with editing for Fantasia Divinity Magazine, where she's gotten to work with many talented authors from all over the world. While she loves to create dark worlds and diverse characters, her greatest creations of all are her sons, Max and Liam, who keep her feet on the ground even while her head is in the clouds.
Website: ambermsimpson.com
Facebook: authorambermsimpson

Cyclops Seeks Soulmate
by Brian Rosenberger

He sits alone, save for his pets and a nearly empty bottle. It's not the first bottle of the night. This is how he spends most evenings.

His pets, the sheep, offer little comfort. The bottle offers even less. He knows he should get out more, maybe do some sightseeing, spend more time gardening. Instead, he sits with his loneliness, the true destroyer.

Polyphemus, the son of Poseidon, deserves better.

Then inspiration.

He pens a personal ad.

Giant heart. Self-employed. A foodie with a taste for the exotic. Enjoys wine and the ocean. Likes animals.

Greek fisherman, not so much.

__Brian Rosenberger__ lives in a cellar in Marietta, GA (USA) and writes by the light of captured fireflies. He is the author of As the Worms Turns and three poetry collections. He is also a featured contributor to the Pro-Wrestling literary collection, Three-Way Dance, available from Gimmick Press.
Facebook: HeWhoSuffers

Love Enclosed
by T.A. Ulven

I embraced her tightly, her spindly frame cold and unresponsive, eyes dull and empty. I promised her I'd never let go. Never give up. Ours was an unyielding love; immortal, unbreaking, uncompromising.

"Don't worry, I'll always be here," I whispered.

We didn't mind the sombre voices, the sobbing horde, or the ponderous speech. All that mattered was that we were together. Locked in perpetual partnership.

As the dirt slowly covered our enclosed resting place, I turned to her and kissed her lifeless lips one last time. Soon we'd be together again.

Gasping for breath, dying, I felt nothing but bliss.

T.A.Ulven is a father, husband, and horror fiction writer hailing from the cold mountains of Norway. He became known through his horror persona hyperobscure, primarily posting short stories on the vast writing subreddit of NoSleep. He has since had work published in several anthologies, and will continue to expand his dark universe for as long as people will visit it.
Facebook: hyperobscure
Reddit: hyperobscura

Flash
by Lynn Reicker

A flash, the colour of spring, flitted through the forest. I followed. Parting branches, I spied her—a tiny being, dancing in puddles, laughing. I stepped. She froze. Discovered, I awaited flight or confrontation, but saw only…flickering. I closed my left eye. She remained. I tried the opposite. That's when the truth was revealed.

Her image was burned on my eye. My right eye. Literally.

Chestnut locks flowed beneath a teal tiara, matching the gown below, a permanent cataract in my vision.

Anger? Despair? No. My only desire was to impair my other eye in the exact same way.

Lynn Reicker was born in the beautiful province of New Brunswick, Canada. She now lives in rural Nova Scotia where she is daily inspired by nature. Lynn was previously published in Engen Book's bestselling anthology, "Chillers From the Rock."

She Loves Me
by Annie Percik

I watch her cooking. Each movement precise, confident. Concentration and grace, punctuated by joyous singing along to the radio. I watch her entertaining. Talking, laughing, making sure everyone's glass is full. The perfect hostess. Queen of her domain, ruling with benevolence. I watch her working. The cute frown line forming between her eyebrows. Competence and efficiency. Completing tasks with accuracy and flair. I watch her sleeping. Expression smoothed out by repose. Peaceful and beautiful, dreaming of things just out of reach.

She loves me. I know she loves me. That's why she leaves the curtains open.

So I can watch.

Annie Percik *lives in London with her husband, Dave, where she is revising her first novel whilst working as a University Complaints Officer. She writes a blog about writing and posts short fiction on her website, which is also where all her current publications are listed. She also publishes a photo-story blog, recording the adventures of her teddy—he is much more popular online than she is. She likes to run away from zombies in her spare time.*
Website: www.alobear.co.uk
Blog: aloysius-bear.dreamwidth.org/

Bonded
by Andrea Allison

His rough hands guided hers. "We have to hurry, my love. The sun will rise soon," he said.

"I-I don't know if I can do this." The knife felt heavy in her hands.

"You have to. It's the only way we can be together. We sip the blood of an innocent and we are bonded for eternity." The sun peeked over the horizon, spilling into the dank garage. "Now!"

A tear slid down her cheek as she plunged the knife into the chest. He slipped a straw into the hole and they filled their bellies with warm magic. Soulmates.

Andrea Allison writes and resides in a small Oklahoman town. Her work has appeared in Trembling With Fear, NoSleep Podcast, Speculative 66, Sirens Call Ezine and various anthologies.
Website: www.andreallison.com

She Loved Sunsets
by Stephen Herczeg

We met in the waves. Two young grommets learning to ride, spending all our time together, both in the water and out.

We married, had kids, jobs, house, a life together. We loved to surf, and she loved watching the sun sink beneath the waves.

We grew old. Her mind slipped away first. I'd bring her to the beach and let the sunset spark her memories.

Tonight was the last time.

I took her past the breakers. She joined the sun as it sank beneath the waves. It was the last thing she saw.

I think she's happier this way.

Stephen Herczeg is an IT Geek based in Canberra Australia. He has been writing for over twenty years and has completed a couple of dodgy novels, sixteen feature length screenplays and numerous short stories and scripts. His horror work has featured in Sproutlings, Hells Bells, Below the Stairs, Trickster's Treats #1 and #2, Shades of Santa, Behind the Mask, Beyond the Infinite; The Body Horror Book, Anemone Enemy, Petrified Punks and Beginnings. He has also had numerous Sherlock Holmes stories published through the Belanger Books - Sherlock Holmes anthologies.
Amazon: amazon.com/-/e/B07916SQQS
Facebook: stephenherczegauthor

Ferrymen
by Maura Yzmore

I keep seeking a place, a time, where someone—anyone—knows how to cure you, my love.

Each wormhole I travel reminds me of Styx, the river that separates the dead from the living. To cross, I must pay, but those Ferrymen don't take coins.

I've lost an ear. Most teeth. Gallbladder. Spleen. Half of my fingers. Half of my toes. Testicles. Kidney. Almost all hope.

Then I lost an eye and finally saw there's even less left of you than there is of me.

It's time to cross the real Styx, my love. I have coins for the Ferryman.

Maura Yzmore is a writer and science professor based in the American Midwest. Some of her darker fare can be found in The Molotov Cocktail, Aphotic Realm, Coffin Bell, and elsewhere. Website: maurayzmore.com Twitter: @MauraYzmore

Beck and Call
by D.L. Smith-Lee

My straight friend calls me for help, and I always come running. I love him. I really do.

"Just did something stupid," he says, opening his apartment door.

"People have made worse choices, I'm sure," I say.

He grabs my arm before I step further into the dark of his home.

"Hey…you love me, right?"

My brows furrow.

He walks before me, the heat of his breath caressing my skin.

"Do you love me?" he demands softly, his lips nearly touching mine. I nod. He flips on the lights, unveiling the blood-soaked living room. "Do you *really* love me?"

D.L. Smith-Lee *was born in the shadow of the grand metropolis of Chicago, the city he calls home. A US Navy vet and lifelong lover of horror and dark fantasy, he writes for the love of creation and storytelling.*
Facebook: dlsmithlee

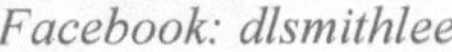

Attracting Love
by Vonnie Winslow Crist

Romance Magnet Oil is easy—two drops of ylang ylang, sandalwood, and clary sage oils, thought Elaine while mixing ingredients to attract love. Selecting a pink candle, she rubbed it with the potion, placed it in a holder, then lit the wick.

After three hours, she snuffed it out. Elaine repeated the spell for eight nights, never blowing out the candle—therefore protecting the fire spirit which resided in its flame and helped facilitate her magic.

On night nine, after the anointed candle was flickering, Elaine heard footsteps.

She smiled, prayed her summoned lover was human, then turned to see.

Vonnie Winslow Crist is author of The Enchanted Dagger, Owl Light, The Greener Forest, Murder on Marawa Prime, and other award-winning books. Her fiction is included in "Amazing Stories," "Cast of Wonders," "Outposts of Beyond," Killing It Softly 2, Defending the Future - Dogs of War, Midnight Masquerade, Chaos of Hard Clay, and elsewhere. A cloverhand who has found so many four-leafed clovers she keeps them in jars, Vonnie strives to celebrate the power of myth in her writing.
Website: www.vonniewinslowcrist.com

Love Potion
by Zoey Xolton

Talena crept to her brother's bedroom and stepped over the tangle of bodies; the result of another gaming night. Her intended target in sight, she crouched down beside him. Seth stirred as she popped the cork on the vial but didn't wake.

"Lucifer has promised me your undying love, in return for my soul. Be my dark knight, and I will be your queen," she whispered, then anointed him with the potion.

In the morning, as she helped herself to breakfast, she felt a pair of hands snake around her waist.

"My queen," Seth whispered into her ear.

Talena smiled.

Zoey Xolton is an Australian Speculative Fiction writer, primarily of Dark Fantasy, Paranormal Romance and Horror. She is also a proud mother of two and is married to her soul mate. Outside of her family, writing is her greatest passion. She is especially fond of short fiction and is working on releasing her own themed collections in future.
Website: www.zoeyxolton.com

Woman's Best Friend
by R.A. Goli

Rowanne knew it was selfish. From the opposite side of the street, she watched as her husband walked their dog, both their heads bowed. She missed her husband too, but he wouldn't see her. Couldn't see her. Bandit would. She called to him.

The dog barked excitedly and bolted across the road, the leash slipping from Eric's loose grip. She looked away.

The blare of a car horn.

The screech of brakes.

Then Bandit was running towards her, tail wagging; his mortal body discarded. Her husband would grieve again, but had his family.

Now she would at least have Bandit.

R.A. Goli is an Australian writer of horror, fantasy, and speculative short stories. In addition to writing, her interests include reading, gaming, the occasional walk, and annoying her dog, two cats, and husband. You can check out her numerous publications including her fantasy novella, The Eighth Dwarf, and her collection of short stories, Unfettered on her website and sign up to her newsletter for free short stories, updates and other fun stuff.
Website: ragoliauthor.wordpress.com/
Facebook: RAGoliAuthor

I Love You, My Angel
by Lynne Phillips

"I love you," are the first words he utters every morning as he gently touches his wife's face. "I'll always love you."

He dresses for work, lightly kisses her. "I love you," he calls as he leaves for work.

On his return, he rushes to her side. He brushes the hair back from her face and lightly gives her a kiss on the lips and tells her about his day.

He marvels at her shiny hair and porcelain skin, it is perfect.

The embalmer was worth the extra money, he thinks.

"I love you my angel," he whispers once more.

Lynne Phillips, a retired teacher, lives in the beautiful Northern Rivers Region of New South Wales Australia. Her stories, across all genres, have been published in anthologies and various online magazines. Her priority is spending time with her family. Her passions are reading, writing and keeping fit.

Personals
by Brian Rosenberger

He sits by the computer, feeling frustrated.

Love was easier then.

Times change. You adapt or disappear.

It's a world of LoversNow.com, Relationships.net, and AffairsAreUs.org.

Questionnaires mix truth with lies. Selfies rarely capture one's true self.

He once worked with a bow and arrow. Ever been struck by an arrow? Hurts like a bitch. An early indicator of the pain you could expect.

Love hurts.

Now it's a cursor, mouse and computer screen. He doesn't worry about the fill-in-the-blank profiles. He closes his eyes and moves the cursor till he feels it.

Love. It's still the will of the Gods.

Brian Rosenberger lives in a cellar in Marietta, GA (USA) and writes by the light of captured fireflies. He is the author of As the Worms Turns and three poetry collections. He is also a featured contributor to the Pro-Wrestling literary collection, Three-Way Dance, available from Gimmick Press.
Facebook: HeWhoSuffers

Simply Love
by Olivia Arieti

Lilian couldn't do without Brian. When he confessed his affair, she swore she wouldn't let self-commiseration or jealousy overwhelm her. If she couldn't win him back, she would accept both. Surprisingly, her husband agreed to such a grotesque farce and the new acquaintance moved in.

The intruder's sly grin was distrustful, and since she shared the bed too, she hid a knife under the mattress.

The price of true love. She smiled while undressing, aware of the bystanders' avid looks.

The nights turned out fun, however, vanity and horror stirred her senses, far better than alone and devoured by resentment.

Olivia Arieti has a degree from the University of Pisa and lives in Torre del Lago Puccini, Italy, with her family. Besides being a published playwright, she loves writing retellings of fairy tales, and at the same time is intrigued by supernatural and horror themes. Her stories appeared in several magazines and anthologies like Enchanted Conversations, Enchanted Tales Literary Magazine, Fantasia Divinity Magazine, Cliterature, Medieval Nightmares, Static Movement, 100 Doors To Madness Forgotten Tomb Press, Black Cats Horrified Press, Bloody Ghost Stories Full Moon Books, Death And Decorations Thirteen O'Clock Press, Infective Ink, Pandemonium Press, Pussy Magic Magazine.

Summer Holidays with Mum and Dad

by Jasmine Jarvis

Every summer, I spend my holiday in my family's cabin in the woods. As I approach the cabin, happy childhood memories flood my mind and fill my heart with love. I walk up the rotted porch stoop, opening the front door. "Mum, Dad, I'm here! I'm home!" I call out in joy. I drop my bag and rush to their bedroom, where I find them lying in bed. I stoop down, kissing them each on their white, cold skulls, their jaws slack in comical grins, their eye sockets vacant. Just as I always remembered them. They haven't changed one bit.

Jasmine Jarvis is a teller of tales and scribbler of scribbles. She lives in Brisbane, Australia with her husband Michael, their two children, Tilly and Mish; Ripley, their German Shepherd, and indoor fat cat, Dwight K. Shrute.

Romance is Dead
by Emma K. Leadley

She wanted flowers and chocolates and romance. Love. But everything she touched turned to dust. She was destined to be alone. She knew who the true love of her life was though; she observed him from the shadows whenever she could. He never knew. Sometimes, he'd give an involuntary shiver and glance over his shoulder, puzzled, but she was careful to stay hidden. Until one day, when he'd taken flowers and chocolates to his new romance, she confronted him. "I love you," she said and kissed him on the lips. His mouth was soft and warm and full of dust.

Emma K. Leadley is a UK-based writer, creative geek, and devourer of words, images and ideas. She began writing both fiction and creative non-fiction as an outlet for her busy brain, and quickly realised scrawling words on a page is wired into her DNA.
Website: emmaleadley.co.uk
Twitter: @autoerraticism

Love and Hope
by Liam Hogan

Sickness howled and death drifted by. Pandora, sobbing in the arms of her husband, caught glimpse of something amid the misery, something bright and unexpected. Maybe what she had just done wasn't all bad, after all.

"What was love doing in that vessel of horrors?"

Epimetheus sighed. "You'd be surprised. Love is terrible because it ends. Love tears people apart. Love is the cruellest of knives."

"Always?"

"Almost always. One in a hundred experience true love."

"One in a hundred?" Pandora echoed, nestling closer, pulse slowing.

And that, Epimetheus thought bitterly, *was why hope was the worst evil of all.*

Liam Hogan is a London based short story writer, the host of Liars' League, and a Ministry of Stories mentor. His story "Ana", appears in Best of British Science Fiction 2016 (NewCon Press) and his twisted fantasy collection, "Happy Ending Not Guaranteed", is published by Arachne Press. Website: happyendingnotguaranteed.blogspot.co.uk Twitter: @LiamJHogan

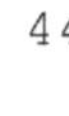

A Single Moment
by Annie Percik

Time and vision shrink to a single point of focus. My entire existence has been building up to this one moment. I see it coming and I'm ready. I appreciate its significance and its impact even as I start to move. The world will remember my sacrifice and praise my bravery. But I don't care about the world. I only care about the girl crossing the street a few steps in front of me. I reach out to her and shove, placing myself in the path of the oncoming bus. I imagine her tears and her pain, and I smile.

Annie Percik lives in London with her husband, Dave, where she is revising her first novel whilst working as a University Complaints Officer. She writes a blog about writing and posts short fiction on her website, which is also where all her current publications are listed. She also publishes a photo-story blog, recording the adventures of her teddy—he is much more popular online than she is. She likes to run away from zombies in her spare time.
Website: www.alobear.co.uk
Blog: aloysius-bear.dreamwidth.org/

All Lovers Were Strangers Once
by Shelly Jarvis

"Hey, Mrs. Tucker. How's it going today?"

I look up from my needlepoint and force a smile. "Fine, Mary. Thanks for asking."

"No change I see."

I shake my head. "No. But I still trust the Lord to deliver him from this coma."

"I hope so, Mrs. Tucker. I'll be praying for you."

As the nurse leaves, I feel the corners of my lips tip up in a smile. She was the hard one to convince, but now, like the rest, she believes me.

"Nothing will interfere with our love," I whisper, leaning over the stranger they call Mr. Tucker.

Shelly Jarvis is a speculative fiction author from West Virginia, US. She found a life-long love of sci-fi and fantasy in the 3rd grade when she found Madeleine L'Engle's "A Wrinkle in Time." Shelly is an avid reader, a Whovian, the ideal viewer of dog rescue videos, and undoubtedly Ravenclaw. She currently has three YA sci-fi books available for purchase on Amazon. Website: www.ShellyJarvis.com

Skin Deep
by Maxine Churchman

Her smooth ebony skin was the first thing that drew his attention. He was a tanner, after all. Then he saw her eyes, so dark and mysterious, and he had to possess her.

Their first date suggested their personalities were incompatible, but he couldn't forget how beautiful her silky skin felt beneath his fingers.

Her eyes pleaded with him from the missing person's picture. A photo couldn't do them justice.

Inside the jar, her eyes had lost none of their mystery. He caressed the silky ebony cushion. It would have been a waste to allow such gorgeous skin to age.

Maxine Churchman lives in Essex UK and has recently started writing poetry and short stories to share. Her interests include learning to improve her writing, reading, knitting, walking and teaching yoga. She is also planning a novel.

Bitter Greetings
by Ximena Escobar

Searching for the words to write about love, she couldn't help the fluster of hurt rising; the curses swelling like a wave on her tongue; the fingers tightening around her pen like a fist readying to punch the mirror where, too often, she'd shift her pupils onto his reflection, always in the corner of the looking glass, instead of admiring her own. It was always about him. Even now, as she tried to drown her anger in that rising tide of resentment, so she could find the words to write something other than

Happy Anniversary!

With love,

From your Amanda.

Ximena Escobar is writing stories and poetry. Originally from Chile, she is the author of a translation into Spanish of the Broadway Musical "The Wizard of Oz", and of an original adaptation of the same, "Navidad en Oz", both produced in her home country. Since 2018 she has published several short stories in various anthologies and online platforms, and is now slowly working on her own collection. Ximena has a degree in Arts & Communication Science and lives in Nottingham with her family.
Facebook: Ximenautora
Twitter: @laximenin

With a Wink in a Blink
by Michael D. Davis

Love only took a few looks, a few minutes to grow. It was the world's fastest blooming flower, the Universe's ever bright star. With a wink, it can be born, and in a blink, it can die. There is nothing faster here or anywhere else faster than love.

Meredith and me had that quick love. For her, I'd do anything, she'd just have to ask. Put a question mark at the end of whatever it is she wants and then just consider it done. That's how I got here. Love, a question mark, and murder has me behind these bars.

Michael D. Davis was born and raised in a small town in the heart of Iowa. Having written over thirty short stories, ranging in genre from comedy to horror from flash fiction to novella he continues in his accursed pursuit of a career in the written word.

The End
by David Bowmore

I love you. You love me too—I know you do.

After more than twenty years, you are essential to my every heartbeat.

And I still only want to be with you.

But the pressure.

The banks won't give us another mortgage and it's their fault, but we're the ones getting the blame. We're the ones who are going to be homeless. Where are we going to find £150k?

I can't continue. No one can help.

I won't force you to come with me, my love. However, there's enough tranquilliser to kill two horses here.

I'll see you in heaven.

David Bowmore *has lived here, there and everywhere, but now lives in Yorkshire with his wonderful wife and a small white poodle. He has worn many hats in his time; head chef, teacher and landscape gardener. His first collection of short stories 'The Magic of Deben Market' is available from Clarendon House.*
Website: davidbowmore.co.uk
Facebook: davidbowmoreauthor

Graphite Rings
by Matt Walker

At 11:36am, she asked him for a pencil.

Annabelle.

Is it inappropriate to offer someone a ring when they ask for a writing utensil? Was it the way she wore her hair like a cape or the way she dressed like a freelance survivor and doodled like a Lovecraftian Dr. Seuss? The way her caustic laugh lied about the smirk in her eye. How do you tell a girl in need of a pencil that you're ready to die of wrinkles by her side?

How do you loan out a pencil and your whole heart at the same time?

Matt Walker is a wandering Vermonter currently working on a myriad of English, Theatre and Philosophy degrees at Franciscan University of Steubenville. When he's not talking someone out of their pizza or planning an ill-fated skydiving extravaganza, he can be found throwing snowballs in the Vatican square or reciting Oscar Wilde on the curb. An accomplished landscaper, farm hand, bouncer and thespian, Walker's travelled extensively across the globe, studying abroad in both China and Central Europe but never managed to visit Nebraska.

Fifty-five Years
by Eddie D. Moore

The celebration in the Banquet Hall of the South Haven Hotel was lively. Adam was working the front desk and smiled as an elderly gentleman slipped out the main door and took a seat in the lobby. After a few moments of consideration, Adam sat down beside the old man.

"Good evening, Mr. Darby. I just wanted to offer my congratulations. Fifty-five years of marriage is quite an accomplishment. What's the secret?"

The old man twitched, and his eyes shifted nervously toward the Banquet Hall doors before answering. "Always keep your guns unloaded and don't die, or else she'll win."

Eddie D. Moore travels hundreds of hours a year, and he fills that time by listening to audiobooks. When he isn't playing with his grandchildren, he writes his own stories. You can find a list of his publications on his blog or by visiting his Amazon Author Page. While you're there, be sure to pick up a copy of his mini-anthology Misfits & Oddities.
Website: eddiedmoore.wordpress.com
Amazon: amazon.com/author/eddiedmoore

Love Isn't What It Used to Be
by Paula R.C. Readman

"I love you, Collin," Daisy said with a childish giggle, "with all my heart and soul."

Collin wondered what her love looked like.

He slipped his hand into her chest cavity, tugged out her heart with a squelch, and held it up to the full moon like it was an offering.

"That doesn't look like love to me," Collin placed his knee on Daisy's ribcage to steady himself before sawing the top of her head off.

"Her love must be hiding in here, with her soul." Collin found nothing recognisable as the grey matter slid onto the blood soaked ground.

Paula R.C. Readman learnt 'How to Write' from books which her husband purchased from eBay. After 250 purchases, he finally told her 'just to get on with the writing'. Since 2010, she's had 34 stories published.
Blog: paulareadman1.wordpress.com

Last Kiss
by C.L. Williams

Lauren and Luis have been forbidden from being together. Wanting to be together, Lauren makes a bold suggestion.

"If we can't be together in life, we'll be together in death!" she says.

"I've got an idea," Luis responds.

Luis reveals a vile of poison and suggests Lauren places the poison upon her lips, he will proceed to kiss her and the two will be able to be in love in a different life.

Lauren does as Luis says; she opens the poison, places it upon her lips, and proceeds to passionately kiss Luis. The two begin to fade, lips locked.

C.L. Williams is an international best-selling author currently living in central Virginia. He has written eight poetry books, four novellas, one novel, and a contributor to a multitude of anthologies and magazines. His most recent anthology appearance ANGELS: Dark Drabbles #2 from Black Hare Press became a number one in hot new releases. C.L. Williams is currently working on his second novel and a new poetry book. Facebook: writer434
Twitter: @writer_434

A Painted Lady
by Clint Foster

I love the way he paints me. I'm jealous of the canvas as his brush drags over it, leaving behind the tones of my own lips, skin, eyes, and hair. Does he love me more than her? Does he love me at all? My smile is chiselled on my face, unmoving, unwavering, and I scarcely blink. I know it will never be good enough for him, but I try harder, nonetheless. He chides me with his eyes before they soften to see his painting. He loves the woman on the canvas. I strive to be perfect like her.

Clint Foster *lives with his herd of four cats, beloved Basset, Zero, and wonderful wife, Nik. He loves to tell stories just as much as he loves to read them, and is excited to share his work. A longtime consumer of media of all kinds, he enjoys giving back what he hopes everyone else thinks are good stories. Facebook: ClintFosterAuthor*

Love Burns
by Andrew Anderson

Harold thought he was being clever; building an ugly-looking folly on the estate which secretly housed his mistress Eve. He claimed it held his collection of rare books, and his wife Louisa was not a reader.

He could privately visit Eve, knowing that Louisa wanted nothing to do with the eyesore or its disclosed contents.

When it burned down one evening, Louisa found Harold crying uncontrollably in the study.

"Harold, you're heartbroken over some silly old books? You're rich—just build another monstrosity to house all your most precious things."

Which she would also burn, if he tried that again.

Andrew Anderson is a spare-time writer of microfiction, flash fiction and short stories, from Bathgate, Scotland. His work has been published on FlashFlood and Re:Written, and published in Black Hare Press anthologies.
Twitter: soorploom

Puppy Love
by J.S. Carnes

"One drink and you become the object of her affection," the old lady said.

Several hours later, Geoffrey sat across from Julia, empty vial in pocket.

Julia gave Geoffrey a polite smile.

"Hey, I…" Geoffrey felt his body tighten.

"Is everything ok? You're sweating. I'll get some water." Julia left the room.

Geoffrey's bones creaked, a throbbing pain in his head followed. Confusion set in, with a…

With a need to shake his butt.

Julia reappeared in the doorway looking every which way.

She looked down.

"Woof!" Geoffrey declared.

Julia looked down, seeing the object of her affection.

"Woof! Woof!"

J.S. Carnes enjoys the sights and sounds of Austin, TX. He enjoys good music, good coffee, good spirits, and good people. He finds inspiration from the unique places he's experienced and the quirky people he's interacted with, then throws in a twist.
Twitter: @JSCarnesAuthor

Dripping Meat
by Hari Navarro

I took her from the street. I knew she would not be missed. I was looking for something. Something painstakingly deciphered from the slick of transmissions you let drift out into the great seething electronic fog.

Something precious that I did not have or, at least, didn't know how to define.

Uncovered in your art, your music, and in strange symbols you attach to messages.

I tear away her filthy rags and strap her to your kitchen table. I slice her flesh and reach into the fevered swell of her chest.

"This beating pulp, this dripping meat…is this…love?"

Hari Navarro has, for many years now, been locked in his neighbours cellar. He survives due to an intravenous feed of puréed extreme horror and Absinthe infused sticky-spiced unicorn wings. His anguished cries for help can be found via 365 Tomorrows, Breachzine, AntipodeanSF, Horror Without Borders, Black Hare Press and HellBound books. Hari was the Winner of the Australasian Horror Writers' Association [AHWA] Flash Fiction Award 2018 and has, also, succeeded in being a New Zealander who now lives in Northern Italy with no cats.
Amazon: amazon.com/Hari-Navarro
Tumblr: harinavarro.tumblr.com

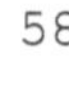

Till Death Do Us Part
by Kathy Slater Neilsen

"I love you," he whispers softly into her ear. Absently, she bats his whisper away, turns and settles deep into her pillow.

One tear falls.

"I love you," he yells as she drives away.

Listening to their favourite song, she sees nothing in the rearview mirror.

"I love you," he declares.

She's consumed with grief, staring at a framed photograph. She's been holding it for hours.

"I love you," she says.

She lays a large bouquet of flowers on his grave.

"I love you too." He looks deeply into her eyes, she sees nothing.

She leaves. He watches her go.

Kathy Slater Neilsen has always possessed a passion for writing as well as reading. Her early writing career included freelance non-fiction. Then, as is often the case, life lead her on a different journey that included motherhood and a small business. But she never stopped writing. Now retired and living on the east coast she is currently writing fiction and is focused on short stories and flash fiction.

Justification
by A.R. Johnston

It's not stalking. Really, it's not. At least, I don't think it is. I'm watching. I take notice of everything that she does. Quietly following her on all her social media. That's not doing anything wrong. Right? That's just staying apprised of what she's doing. Nothing creepy; I'm not standing outside her window, staring in. Well...across the street with my telescope, but that's different. Is it my fault that she moved in next door and my telescope just happened to swing that way? No, of course not. I'm just watching out for her is all. Not stalking at all.

A.R. Johnston is a small-town girl from Nova Scotia, Canada. She is known to write mostly urban fantasy, though she goes where the muses lead her and you never know where that may be. She is a lover of coffee, good tv shows, horror flicks, and a reader of good books. She pretends to be a writer when real life doesn't get in the way. Pesky full-time job and adulting!
Facebook: arjohnstonauthor
Website: arjohnstonauthor.wordpress.com

Crushed
by Shawn M. Klimek

Georgette couldn't believe her long-time admirer had brought flowers to their coffee meet up. "How sweet," she said, uncomfortably.

"I've had a crush on you for the longest time," Jerome revealed. "I wanted to make this moment something we could tell our kids."

They both laughed but Georgette died a little inside.

Sensing something amiss, Jerome challenged, "We are here to plan our first date, aren't we?"

"It's just a party at some guy's house," she said. "I only need you there long enough to throw his girlfriend off the scent. With any luck, I won't need a ride home."

Shawn M. Klimek is the middle child of seven creative siblings, a globetrotting, U.S. military spouse, an internationally best-selling short-story writer, award-winning poet, and butler to a Maltese. More than one hundred and fifty of his stories and poems have been published in digital magazines or anthologies, including BHP's Deep Space, Eerie Christmas and every book so far in the Dark Drabbles series.
Website: jotinthedark.blogspot.com
Facebook: shawnmklimekauthor

We Love You, Aubrey
by Jasmine Jarvis

"I don't like it here, Alfie," I whisper. "I'm scared." Alfie places his paw on my shoulder, "You will be okay. We are here with you, no one can hurt you anymore. We love you, Aubrey."

I look up and see my friends, Alfie Cat and Bertie Bunny. They smile at me. "I love you too. We had to get rid of the Bad Man, didn't we?"

My friends nod.

***

"What is the patient doing now?" asks the psychiatrist.

The nurse looks at the monitor and replies, "Patient is sitting on the floor of her room talking to herself again."

Jasmine Jarvis is a teller of tales and scribbler of scribbles. She lives in Brisbane, Australia with her husband Michael, their two children, Tilly and Mish; Ripley, their German Shepherd, and indoor fat cat, Dwight K. Shrute.

Cupid's Cruel Bow
by Monica Schultz

Kadin watches her glow from the back of the classroom. The sunshine glistens in Chloe's golden hair, highlighting every perfect strand.

Thump.

Cupid's bow strikes him down. Splitting his chest open with pure light.

"Kadin?"

The teacher's fingers snap before his eyes, bringing the class to attention.

"I asked you a question?"

A chorus of giggles erupt at the sight of his blank face. Chloe turns. Her brilliant blue eyes are another arrow piercing his flesh. A flawless friend leans close to whisper in her ear.

Thump.

Her cruel smile slays with ease, securing Cupid's arrow in his wounded heart.

Monica Schultz is a full-time Mathematics and History teacher from Ipswich, Australia, with a passion for writing fantasy. When she isn't busy finding 'x' in the latest equation, you can find her curled up with a young adult book and a cat on her lap. Website: https://monicaschultzauthor.weebly.com/ Instagram: @monicaschultzauthor

For the Best
by J.W. Garrett

Bethany crept closer to the window. If she closed her eyes, she could imagine herself with David instead of the imposter inside. The nights they'd spent together… Did his wife know?

She'd make sure of it.

Bethany, knocked, entered. Confused, she joined David and the imposter. The two women shared a glance.

"Wine?" she asked.

Bethany nodded, sipped, drank again. She lifted her eyes, meeting David's hardened gaze.

It's for the best that she knows.

Bethany opened her mouth, but words wouldn't come. Her throat clenched, spasmed. She gasped for breath, sputtering, spilling wine.

"Best for all, Bethany." David winked.

J.W. Garrett has been writing in one form or another since she was a teenager. She currently lives in Florida with her family but loves the mountains of Virginia where she was born. Her writings include YA fantasy as well as short stories. Since completing Remeon's Quest-Earth Year 1930, the prequel in her YA fantasy series, Realms of Chaos, she has been hard at work on the next in the series, scheduled to release August 2020. When she's not hanging out with her characters, her favourite activities are reading, running and spending time with family.
Website: www.jwgarrett.com
BHC Press: www.bhcpress.com/Author_JW_Garrett.html

First Date
by Patrick Winters

It was an incredible day.

We lay on the blanket, our bare feet tickling along the grass for hours.

She would lay back as I leaned over her, staring into that gorgeous face while I fed her dainty grapes.

I told her things that I had never dared to tell anyone else. I even got to crying, and when I did, she told me everything was okay. And she made me believe it.

It was so wonderful.

And as the sun finally set, I put her back in her casket, filled up the hole, and left with a lighter heart.

Patrick Winters is a graduate of Illinois College in Jacksonville, IL, where he earned a Bachelor of Arts degree in English Literature and Creative Writing and achieved membership into Sigma Tau Delta, an international English honors society. Winters is now a proud member of the Horror Writers Association, and his work has been published in the likes of Sanitarium Magazine, Deadman's Tome, Trysts of Fate, and other such titles. A full list of his previous publications may be found at his author's site.
Website: wintersauthor.azurewebsites.net/Publications/List

Poison Heart
by Terry Miller

Love is a delicate tapestry, woven in interlocking strands until something beautiful is created. Unfortunately, if a strand loosens, it begins to fall apart. When did emotions become so dependent upon perfection? What hope is there for mending? Ashley hadn't a clue.

She lay beside B.J., his skin beginning to pull away from its seams. The perfect boyfriend was rare; Ashley was lucky to have found the desired parts. He wasn't much for conversation, but he was such a great listener. As the poison took effect, she laid her head on his bare chest. Soon she would be with him.

Terry Miller lives in Portsmouth, Ohio. His work has been featured in Sanitarium Magazine, Devolution Z, Jitter, Rhysling Anthology 2017, Poetry Quarterly, Sirens Call Ezine, The Horror Tree's Trembling With Fear, SpillWords, Organic Ink Vol. I, Curses & Cauldrons Anthology from Blood Song Books, Forest of Fear from Blood Song Books, the Dark Drabble Anthology Series from Black Hare Press, 100 Word Zombie Bites from Reanimated Writers Press, Scary Snippets, Guilty Pleasures & Other Dark Delights, 100 Word Horrors 3, and O Unholy Night In Deathlehem from Grinning Skull Press.
Facebook: tmiller2015
Amazon: amazon.com/author/millerterryl

Ancient Bandages
by Matthew M. Montelione

Cold rain soaked through Necho's ancient bandages to his cursed skin. He stared longingly at Helen through the window panes. She brushed her soft brown hair. Safe. Warm. Dry. Oblivious to his existence.

The mummy cried on the inside; he loved her so much. He knew who she really was: the reincarnation of his long-lost love. For now, he waited. Helen was young and full of life. She would have to die to be with him.

Necho moaned and limped away, dragging his muddy feet across the saturated lawn.

Helen suddenly turned towards the window, but saw only pouring rain.

Matthew M. Montelione is a horror writer and American Revolution historian born and raised on Long Island in New York. His work has been published in many titles, including MONSTERS: A Horror Microfiction Anthology, Quoth the Raven: A Contemporary Reimagining of the Works of Edgar Allan Poe, Thuggish Itch: Devilish, WHAT IF?: History Rewritten, Long Island History Journal, and Journal of the American Revolution. Matthew lives with his wife in New York. Website: maybeevils.com Facebook: maybeevils

The Hunt
by Zoey Xolton

Elizabeth quickened her pace. The hour was late. The wind rustled the leaves on the trees and kicked up debris on the street. The nightlife in the city was exhilarating, but she preferred the quiet of the suburbs.

*****

David watched the woman from afar, as he had for months. Every weekend it was the same, predictable routine. Now was his chance. Through the shadows he crept, until he could smell her perfume.

Pouncing upon his prey—the tables turned. Slammed to the ground, he looked up at the woman in the red dress. She smiled, revealing her fangs.

"Hello, handsome."

Zoey Xolton *is an Australian Speculative Fiction writer, primarily of Dark Fantasy, Paranormal Romance and Horror. She is also a proud mother of two and is married to her soul mate. Outside of her family, writing is her greatest passion. She is especially fond of short fiction and is working on releasing her own themed collections in future.*
Website: www.zoeyxolton.com

Pieces of You
by J.S. Carnes

"Act like a lady." Sandy's hand grazed over her wedding dress. "Or die alone."

How she'd dreamed of this day!

"No matter. They were right." Sandy turned to her patchwork groom. "Best of you all."

She laughed, tracing her fingers across cut-outs of the perfect man; eyes, nose, face, body.

"Nobody's perfect." Sandy gazed into Todd's baby blue eyes and kissed the edge of John's frozen grin, each swollen lip sewn onto Stephen's face with velvet thread. "Isn't that right? Do have to say, learning to sew paid off."

The oven timer sounded, "Oh, and cooking. Hun, Jerry's liver's ready!"

J.S. Carnes enjoys the sights and sounds of Austin, TX. He enjoys good music, good coffee, good spirits, and good people. He finds inspiration from the unique places he's experienced and the quirky people he's interacted with, then throws in a twist.
Twitter: @JSCarnesAuthor

Punch Me, My Love
by Carole de Monclin

The bruise on my thigh has almost faded away. My arm and knee still display explosions of red and purple hues. Whatever people think of our marriage, I never hide my bruises.

Fingers slither around my neck from behind.

For a second, I wait, experiencing the pressure on my windpipe. Not worse than what he's done to me before.

My hands surge and pluck away the fingers. I whirl around, elbow raised, aiming at the nose. He blocks. I groan and knee him.

"Careful, Lovebirds," the self-defence instructor chuckles.

Our enthusiasm's famous, always going all out, but never too far.

Carole de Monclin travels both the real world and imaginary ones. She's lived in France, Australia, and the USA; visited 25+ countries; and explored Mars, Ceres, and many distant planets. She writes to invite people on a journey. Her stories can be found in The Arcanist, The Deep Space Anthology, and every volume of the Dark Drabbles series.
Website: CaroledeMonclin.com
Twitter: @CaroledeMonclin

Valentine Heart
by Radar DeBoard

Mark placed the wrapped Valentine's present in front of Taylor's locker, then raced around the corner at the sound of footsteps. He felt a large group of butterflies in his stomach as he walked down the hall.

He had been in love with Taylor ever since the third grade, he'd just never had the guts to make a move himself. That was before he found out that Andrew Gilbert had been cheating on her.

Well, Mark would be there to comfort and give Taylor all of his heart. As well as Andrew's heart, all wrapped up with a nice bow.

Radar DeBoard is a horror movie and novel enthusiast who resides in the small town of Goddard, Kansas. He occasionally dabbles in writing, and enjoys to make dark tales for people to enjoy. He has had drabbles and short stories published in various electronic magazines and anthologies.
Facebook: WriterRadarDeBoard

1963

by David Bowmore

Strange, I thought I could live without her. But her image is everywhere. The films will always be there. There was no one like her.

I dream about her more than ever, taunting me with her breathy voice and come to bed eyes. But now those eyes are dead, and worms fall from her pale lips.

I thought I might be able to cope with the guilt, but I cannot go on anymore.

Everything is in place. My assassination will be the greatest cover up in history.

The American public will always remember my sacrifice.

They will always love me.

David Bowmore *has lived here, there and everywhere, but now lives in Yorkshire with his wonderful wife and a small white poodle. He has worn many hats in his time; head chef, teacher and landscape gardener. His first collection of short stories 'The Magic of Deben Market' is available from Clarendon House.*
Website: davidbowmore.co.uk
Facebook: davidbowmoreauthor

Desert Wind
by Vonnie Winslow Crist

Beneath Arizona's moon, Patti dreamed of desert wind—its breath on her neck, its fingers combing her hair.

Her fascination didn't diminish with daybreak. Rather, she craved the touch of gritty air laden with the scent of cactus.

No longer able to resist, she went outside, closed eyes, focused on dust devils, and took a deep breath.

Whistling up the wind, Patti wished for someone who loved the dry heat as much as she.

Suddenly, she felt lips pressed against hers.

Opening eyes, Patti saw she'd summoned not a man, but a demon—hot as hellfire and her perfect mate.

Vonnie Winslow Crist is author of The Enchanted Dagger, Owl Light, The Greener Forest, Murder on Marawa Prime, and other award-winning books. Her fiction is included in "Amazing Stories," "Cast of Wonders," "Outposts of Beyond," Killing It Softly 2, Defending the Future - Dogs of War, Midnight Masquerade, Chaos of Hard Clay, and elsewhere. A cloverhand who has found so many four-leafed clovers she keeps them in jars, Vonnie strives to celebrate the power of myth in her writing.
Website: www.vonniewinslowcrist.com

Motherly Love
by J.U. Menon

Edwina was, for all intents and purposes, a cuddly teddy bear. Her soft brown eyes and friendly smile belied the deep hurt she felt inside—she had been separated from her baby at the toy factory, years before.

"Alia, your dinner's getting cold!"

"Coming, Mummy!"

The little girl crossed the room towards her teddy bear. Edwina had come to love Alia as her own child. She smiled, a hint of fang catching the light from the corridor. She couldn't wait to sink her teeth into Alia's soft skin. She would then transform into a baby bear and be Edwina's forever.

J.U. Menon is a scientist living in Rhode Island, USA, and is currently working on her young adult novel. She writes fantasy and science fiction while occasionally dabbling in dark fiction and poetry.
Twitter: @ju_menon
Instagram: @iam_jumenon

Love Among the Sand Dunes
by Paula R.C. Readman

That summer, so long ago. The wind tugged at your hair while your eyes sparkled. I tried not to stare.

"You're so good to me, Johnny," you said, so breathlessly. It made my heart ache.

I was just a good friend. Someone to fill your empty days as you waited for your lover's return.

I couldn't allow it to happen. Not when my love was far greater.

My heart raced as I rubbed the lotion on your bare shoulders. With ease, my fingertips caressed your throat, and then I tightened them.

Now my love lies buried beneath the sand dunes.

Paula R.C. Readman learnt 'How to Write' from books which her husband purchased from eBay. After 250 purchases, he finally told her 'just to get on with the writing'. Since 2010, she's had 34 stories published.
Blog: paulareadman1.wordpress.com

Until Death
by Shawn M. Klimek

Radiant in white before the altar, holding her intended's hand, Candace stared into his eager eyes as the priest solemnly recited their vows in Old Latin.

"I do!" Evan answered when asked.

Candace listened as the recitation resumed, gravely awaiting her turn to speak. When the moment arrived, however, she hesitated, glassy eyed and trembling. Something felt wrong.

Someone whispered, "Is she waking up at last?"

Candace felt Evan squeeze her hand impatiently.

"I do," Candace, surrendered.

Relieved, the witnesses applauded.

Pronouncing the ceremony complete, the priest proceeded to assist Candace out of her linen gown and onto the altar.

Shawn M. Klimek is the middle child of seven creative siblings, a globetrotting, U.S. military spouse, an internationally best-selling short-story writer, award-winning poet, and butler to a Maltese. More than one hundred and fifty of his stories and poems have been published in digital magazines or anthologies, including BHP's Deep Space, Eerie Christmas and every book so far in the Dark Drabbles series.
Website: jotinthedark.blogspot.com
Facebook: shawnmklimekauthor

Unknown Eyes
by Peter J. Foote

<<Open port to LeggieLucie83?>> glows on the screen.

A figure hunches over the keyboard, types a steady rhythm. In seconds a bank of monitors light up.

Every wireless device in Lucinda Montague's apartment powers on; her laptop, tablet, phone, gaming systems, and even cameras she doesn't know about, thanks to a blackmailed superintendent.

The figure watches the feeds for hours as they show the various glimpses of Lucinda's life; as she does yoga, showers, cooks, talks on her phone and lives her life, unaware that greedy eyes watch it all.

"My little Lucy, how I missed you," the figure says.

Peter J. Foote is a bestselling speculative fiction writer from Nova Scotia. Outside of writing, he runs a used bookstore specialising in fantasy & sci-fi, cosplays, and alternates between red wine and coffee as the mood demands. His short stories can be found in both print and in ebook form, with his story "Sea Monkeys" winning the inaugural "Engen Books/Kit Sora, Flash Fiction/Flash Photography" contest in March of 2018. As the founder of the group "Genre Writers of Atlantic Canada", Peter believes that the writing community is stronger when it works together.
Twitter: @PeterJFoote1
Website: peterjfooteauthor.wordpress.com

The Embrace
by Michael Crow

Their short time together was intense, but he fell for her… Baby dolly pallor contrasted beautifully with her pumpkin-coloured hair. She lay starkers, at perfect peace. Forget-me-not blue eyes looked up, wide-open, indifferent to her surroundings.

The fresh, purple scars only made her more seductive. A lightning thrill shot up his spine, heart raced, and he felt warm snugness below. His heart thudded like a drum as he went to touch her. One more lover's embrace. Cold as a Minnesota winter.

"Daryl! Get her off the slab, the autopsy is finished. The undertaker will be here soon to fetch her."

Michael Crow spends his sparse free time writing about sports, as well as working on his own fiction. Michael is the owner of Real Dead Review, a blog devoted to dark fiction. Michael's non-fiction works have appeared on USA Today, Fansided Network, The Guillotine, and Intermat. Michael makes his home with his wife, daughter and two cats in Central Minnesota.

For Better or For Worse
by D.J. Elton

They had been childhood sweethearts before the war. Each year binding themselves together in fresh red blood, brothers of blood, their own sacred ritual. Now it was post-wartime, and Nila and Paru had been separated—not in the flesh, but by religion and their family's customs and systems.

Nila sat in a rickety wheelchair with her remaining two limbs working their hands hard to face Paru, her life-bonded one. Paru held her back, gently touched her neck, whispering words that meant love, although now he could not remember her name, let alone yesterday. Always bonded, they together left the mortal realm.

***D.J. Elton** is a writer living in Melbourne's west. As a child she came from England to Australia, on the last boat down the Suez Canal, where she underwent a sacrificial dunking ritual in the court of King Neptune, and has never looked back. She likes creating speculative micro fiction and short stories, as well as random essays. Her work has been published in several anthologies, and she has written a historical fantasy novella, 'The Merlin Girl.' When not playing with a pen, she likes most of all to go to the green country.*

Let's Pretend
by Nicola Currie

Sarah is adorable. Being in a relationship with her is like playing a game; I think she can't get cuter, then she levels up.

Last week, as I picked up my step to catch-up with her when she got off the bus, she glanced behind then hid herself in one of the shops around the corner so I'd have to search, like we were infants playing hide and seek.

Now, finding me in her apartment, she screams, playing a damsel that needs rescuing.

"Who are you?" she pretends, eyes wide like a Disney princess. "What do you want?"

So adorable.

Nicola Currie is from Cambridge, UK where she works in educational publishing. She has published poetry in literary magazines, including Mslexia and Sarasvati, and short stories in various anthologies. She has also completed her first novel, which was longlisted for the Bath Children's Novel Award. Website: writeitandweep.home.blog

The Harvest
by Rowanne S. Carberry

"Please," they beg, "don't do this."

"I'm sorry." Tears fill my eyes. It needs to be done.

Placing the mask over their mouths muffles their protests. The gas knocks them out. I breathe a sigh of relief as their struggles end. I don't want to cause pain.

Finally, I wheel in the tray that's loaded with the instruments I need.

I don't know how much time passes before I'm ready to pick up the phone.

"Mum… I got it."

Looking down at the heart surrounded by ice, I close the lid, grab the box, and head to the transplant unit.

Rowanne S. Carberry *was born in England in 1990, where she stills lives now with her cat Wolverine. Rowanne has always loved writing, and her first poem was published at the age of 15, but her ambition has always been to help people. Rowanne studied at the University of Sunderland where she completed combined honours of Psychology with Drama. Rowanne writes to offer others an escape. Although Rowanne writes in varied genres each story or poem she writes will often have a darkness to it, which helped coin her brand, Poisoned Quill Writing – Wicked words from a poisoned quill.*
Facebook: PoisonedQuillWriting
Instagram: @poisoned_quill_writing

No One Loves
by Raven Corinn Carluk

"Anna. You've found me." He sounded as surprised as she'd ever heard. Meaning not at all.

She glared, knife clenched, heart racing and stomach churning. Anna daren't think his name, he whom had tormented her for a year. Kept her in a cage. Threatened to kill her repeatedly. Driven her to murder. He whom had sculpted her through sociopathic stagings, one after the other.

He whom she couldn't live without.

Anna dropped the knife and flung herself into his arms. She couldn't tell him how he was the only one who understood. He held her close; she wouldn't have to.

Raven Corinn Carluk *writes dark fantasy, paranormal romance, and anything else that catches her interest. She's authored five novels, where she explores themes of love and acceptance. Her shorter pieces, usually from her darker side, can be found in Black Hare Press anthologies, at Detritus Online, and through Alban Lake Publishers.*
Twitter: @ravencorinn
Website: www.ravencorinncarluk.com

I Love You So Much
by Gabriella Balcom

"She needs a transplant," the doctors said after Maddie's kidneys shut down. But the organ registry had no matches at all. None could be found except for me, and they refused to take mine.

My precious baby is nine and deteriorating rapidly. I was fifty-two when I had her, and her presence changed everything. Her father abandoned us, but she's brought such joy into my life.

"Maddie, I love you so much," I wrote after talking with my sister. My plans horrified her, and she'll arrive soon to try to dissuade me.

When the doorbell rang, I pulled the trigger.

Gabriella Balcom lives in Texas with her family, loves reading and writing, and thinks she was born with a book in her hands. She works in a mental health field, and writes fantasy, horror/thriller, romance, children's stories, and sci-fi. She likes travelling, music, good shows, photography, history, interesting tales, and animals. Gabriella says she's a sucker for a great story and loves forests, mountains, and back roads which might lead who knows where. She has a weakness for lasagne, garlic bread, tacos, cheese, and chocolate, but not necessarily in that order.
Facebook: GabriellaBalcom.lonestarauthor

A Kind of Telenovela Love
by María J. Estrada

The dirty Blueline was not the place. Yet Rosa sat there, longing for warmth and companionship.

He got on at the California stop. He was strong, wearing a clean-cut black suit and adorable kitten socks. The socks caught her eye. His curly soft hair. Cold blue eyes.

He smirked as she sank back into her book.

"My name is Pedro," he said and held out his hand. Her heart skipped a beat. She thought, *Should I take a chance?*

As their fingers connected, she knew; he was the one.

By next weekend, they would be burying bodies in the garden.

María J. Estrada grew up in the desert outside of Yuma, Arizona, in a barrio comprised of new Mexican immigrants and first-generation Chicanos. She has published poetry, fiction, and essays in Overthrowing Capitalism: Volume 6, One Surviving Poem, Poetica, Tempest, Blaze, Spillwords Press, Dastaan World Magazine, and The Inner Circle Writers' Magazine. She lives in Chicago, IL.
Website: barrioblues.com
Twitter: @drmariajestrada

Deserved?
by C.L. Williams

A triggered Cameron slaps Candice as he screams, "Who is he?"

A distraught Candice responds, "I don't know!"

Cameron slaps her once more. "Answer me, or I swear to God, the next hit will be a punch to the face!"

Candice speaks through her tears, "I'm sorry. I love you!"

Cameron pulls his punch back and hits her, blood gushing everywhere. He hurries to the bathroom to grab a towel and helps Candice wipe off the blood.

"Candice," Cameron says, "I love you, but sometimes, you deserve this."

Candice says nothing, she simply lays herself in Cameron's arms.

C.L. Williams is an international best-selling author currently living in central Virginia. He has written eight poetry books, four novellas, one novel, and a contributor to a multitude of anthologies and magazines. His most recent anthology appearance ANGELS: Dark Drabbles #2 from Black Hare Press became a number one in hot new releases. C.L. Williams is currently working on his second novel and a new poetry book.
Facebook: writer434
Twitter: @writer_434

Motherlove
by David M. Donachie

Abigail's heart trembled in her chest; traitorous; failing.

"Don't worry," Carole told her, "a donor is coming."

"How do you know, Mummy?"

The doctors told her that there was little hope. Hearts small enough for a nine-year-old required a tragedy. *But still*, Carole thought, she had always been small herself. It was a simple equation: one life for another.

When they rushed Abigail into surgery, she wondered why her mother wasn't there to hold her hand. When she woke, they tried to break the news gently.

Abigail smiled. "Don't worry, I know that Mummy will always be with me now."

David M. Donachie is an artist, author, and games designer. He has written short stories of countless types since he was old enough to hold a pencil — many are very embarrassing, the others appear in his self-published anthology The Night Alphabet, and in numerous anthologies. He lives in a garret (really a top-floor flat, but a garret sounds a lot more romantic) in Edinburgh with his wife Victoria, two cats, more reptiles than mammals, and more invertebrates than either.

Such is the Drama of Possessive Love
by D.J. Elton

Beloved:

Will you love me to the end of time? Will you die for me? This is the oath. The truth. Will you protect me? Honour me? Adore me? Allow me freedom to be myself? Always? Will you kiss me every day with a passion that is endless? Can I be with you every day? All day? Forever together in our love that keeps growing? Will you support me in everything I say and do?

Then, if not, I will sacrifice myself for our love. I will choose a method, and like Cleopatra, I will let it take me away.

D.J. Elton is a writer living in Melbourne's west. As a child she came from England to Australia, on the last boat down the Suez Canal, where she underwent a sacrificial dunking ritual in the court of King Neptune, and has never looked back. She likes creating speculative micro fiction and short stories, as well as random essays. Her work has been published in several anthologies, and she has written a historical fantasy novella, 'The Merlin Girl.' When not playing with a pen, she likes most of all to go to the green country.

Obsession
by R.J. Meldrum

A gaggle of girls walk past, but I ignore them. I'm waiting for you. I know the bars you frequent, so it's just a matter of time. You appear with a group of your friends. I follow you into the club, straight past the bouncers. No-one can see me. I stand next to you. I reach over and stroke your arm. You frown and touch the spot, as if you felt something. I want to tell you I'm near, but you can't hear me. I want to tell you death is no barrier to love. I will never leave you.

R. J. Meldrum is an author and academic. Born in Scotland, he moved to Ontario, Canada in 2010. He has had stories published by Horrified Press, the Infernal Clock, Trembling with Fear, Darkhouse Books, Smoking Pen Press, and James Ward Kirk Fiction. He also has had stories published in The Sirens Call e-zine, the Horror Zine and Drabblez Magazine. He is an Affiliate Member of the Horror Writers Association.
Twitter: @RichardJMeldru1
Facebook: richard.meldrum.79

Through the Window
by Rowanne S. Carberry

Watching her through the window, his hand slips to his groin. He stares as her top comes off. She'd forgotten to close the curtains again.

His hand squeezes as her bra drops to the floor.

He'd only met her twice, and only for a few short minutes.

But she was his.

Someone else's hands circle her waist, fingers tickling over her bare skin.

His eyes narrow, anger heating his blood.

How dare someone touch what is mine.

Hands move to the small of his back, the metal bringing him back to his senses. He knows what he has to do.

Rowanne S. Carberry was born in England in 1990, where she stills lives now with her cat Wolverine. Rowanne has always loved writing, and her first poem was published at the age of 15, but her ambition has always been to help people. Rowanne studied at the University of Sunderland where she completed combined honours of Psychology with Drama. Rowanne writes to offer others an escape. Although Rowanne writes in varied genres each story or poem she writes will often have a darkness to it, which helped coin her brand, Poisoned Quill Writing – Wicked words from a poisoned quill.
Facebook: PoisonedQuillWriting
Instagram: @poisoned_quill_writing

Bonnie's Last Poem
by J.M. Meyer

Mama said I'm a sucker for bad boys.

I met Clyde while pouring coffee at Hargrave's café. Nineteen and tired of poverty, I welcomed an adventure. Clyde ignored the ring on my ringer, and I pretended his V8 Ford wasn't stolen. We're still alive after two years of robbing and killing.

We knew our love would end in an early death; the mystery was how and when.

A bank robbery didn't kill us, but the betrayal of a friend with a fake broken car did.

Bullets pounded through metal, lashed through glass, and pierced our hearts; destroying our love forever.

J.M. Meyer is a writer, artist and small business owner living in New York, where she received her master's degree from Teachers College, Columbia University. Jacqueline enjoys writing speculative fiction and mysteries. Her favorite author is Alice Munro and her favorite film…is…anything horror related. Jacqueline also enjoys hiking with her dog Molly and the company of her husband Bruce and daughters; Julia, Emma and Lauren. Jacqueline's Mantra lately; there's no such thing as failing, it's called learning.
Website: jmoranmeyer.net
Amazon: www.amazon.com/author/jacquelinemoranmeyer

Purple Hyacinth
by Kaitlyn Arnett

The two stood, face to face, gold meeting silver. The song they danced to was a sombre one, like a record stuck on the same tune. The man was the first to move, bowing deeply with a flourish as he rose. Pulling a purple hyacinth from his jacket, he offered it.

"It truly is a blessing have met you in this lifetime, for you truly are a beauty, Moria."

The dark-skinned woman shot him a venomous glare. "And as always, Felix, I could have gone another century without even thinking of you."

They moved on, the flower left to wilt.

Kaitlyn Arnett is a teen author who has been writing for five years. She focuses on the fantasy and thriller genres, specifically drabbles and short stories.

No More Flowers
by Catherine Kenwell

"No more flowers," she whispered, and pressed her lips to the cold marble.

"It's not enough to allay my loneliness," she continued. "I miss you too much."

She saluted the gravestone with her mickey of Crown Royal and carefully placed a blanket on the grave.

"I'm just going to sit here and keep you company, okay?" she asked the silence as she settled herself, cross-legged on the blanket.

An hour later, she tossed her empty bottle. Two hours on, as dusk approached, she lay across the blanket, sobbing.

Come morning, she had frozen to death, forever tethered to her love.

Catherine Kenwell is a Barrie, Ontario, mediator and author. After 30 successful years in corporate communications, she sustained a brain injury, lost her job, and joined the circus. She writes both horror/dark fiction and inspirational non-fiction. Her works have been published in Chicken Soup for the Soul, Trembling with Fear, Siren's Call, and HellBound Books. Website: www.catherinekenwell.com

Actions Speak Louder
by James Turnbow

I watched my father grip the bat in his hand tightly.

"Do you know the Mvskoke word for love?" he asked me.

"No," I answered.

"We don't have one. Do you know why that is?"

I thought for a few moments.

"I don't. I never thought about it."

He pointed his bat at the quivering figure tied up in the corner of our garage.

"You remember Kyle? He's been hitting your sister again."

My father reared back and delivered a thunderous blow to Kyle's knees and then tossed me the bat.

"We don't *say* I love you. We show it."

James Turnbow is a graduate from the University of Central Oklahoma with a degree in Strategic Communications. He is a proud member of the Seminole Nation of Oklahoma and works with tribal youth to empower them to pursue higher education as an Education Advisor for the Muscogee Creek Nation. He is a curator of Seminole culture and language and works to preserve the stories and words of his ancestors.

Mother's Day
by A.R. Dean

A child is all I've ever wished for. Someone who loves me no matter what. Children worship their mommy.

I don't need anyone to have a baby. My child is out there waiting for me to find it.

It's late at the store when I ram my cart into hers. I apologise and ask about her swollen belly. "Thirty-eight weeks," she answers. "A girl."

I'd like a daughter. Following the woman to the dark parking lot, I cut my baby free. Together baby and I go home.

Alice is four now and wants a sibling. Guess I should go shopping.

A.R. Dean is a dark and twisted soul. Dean has spent their whole life spreading fear with the tales from their head. Best known for stories that terrify and show the evilest side of human nature. So, look for Dean haunting your local cemetery or under your bed, because they're here to spread the fear. Turn off your lights and enjoy a scare. Dean is being published in Black Hare Press's Beyond and Unravel Anthologies. Keep a lookout for more stories.
Facebook: A.R. Dean Author & Ghoul

That Which Lacks a Heart Wants What It Wants
by Raymond Johnson

Death stared at the vibrant colours. They were not colours a mortal eye could see, but rather sparks of emotion. Glowing joy danced before him while dark depression swirled around his feet. The air was heavy with the smell of hope as sadness melted on his tongue.

He was void of these colours, as they could not exist within him, but he wanted them, nonetheless. He cherished life, he longed to hold, caress, and embrace her. He was empty, but she was full. No matter how hard he resisted, he still loved her. With a touch, the light was gone.

***Raymond Johnson** is a funeral director in central Ohio who basically writes horror and Litrpg stories in the little spare time he has. He has five children, a wife, a dog, and a cat and for fun he does a youtube show called the Litrpg Audiobook Podast.*

Gift-Wrapped
by Robin Braid

The pink, heart-shaped note on the table read, "Backyard."

I left the house and followed the crooked path. Another note was pinned to the shed, fluttering in the breeze. "Warm."

With trembling hands, I eased the shed door open. In the gloom of the interior, a large sack sat in the corner and a battered suitcase lay on the floor. On the case was a final note, "All my love. Enjoy xxx."

Inside, metal implements varying in width, length and sharpness gleamed in the leaden light. I picked up a scalpel as the sack began to twitch. Happy Valentine's, baby.

Robin Braid writes stories of the mysterious and macabre. A resident of Fife, Scotland, he graduated from Dundee University with a degree in English Literature. When not working in his regular job he can often be found rambling over hills and glens in search of inspiration for further tales. Twitter: @robinbraid

Love Never Dies
by Lynne Phillips

The old man brings her flowers every day. He sits by her side and softly whispers how much he loves her. The look on his face is a joy to watch.

After lunch, he lies down beside her and sleeps with a smile on his face.

The sun sinks low in the sky as I walk over to remind him I have to lock up soon. It's council policy for the cemetery to be locked at night.

I touch his hand; it is stone cold.

This will be the first time in years he doesn't have to leave her alone.

Lynne Phillips, a retired teacher, lives in the beautiful Northern Rivers Region of New South Wales Australia. Her stories, across all genres, have been published in anthologies and various online magazines. Her priority is spending time with her family. Her passions are reading, writing and keeping fit.

I See You
by Brian Rosenberger

I love that nervous smile you have whenever we meet and how your blue eyes light up in total surprise.

I see you at the laundromat. How meticulously you fold your clothes. Someday you'll be folding mine.

I see you at the gym, the way you glisten as you work out. Someday, I'll taste your sweat.

I see you in your bedroom, in your kitchen, getting your mail.

I see you at the gun range. Target practice has paid off. You've gotten much better. I wanted to compliment you, but you were already gone. No worries.

I'll see you soon.

Brian Rosenberger lives in a cellar in Marietta, GA (USA) and writes by the light of captured fireflies. He is the author of As the Worms Turns and three poetry collections. He is also a featured contributor to the Pro-Wrestling literary collection, Three-Way Dance, available from Gimmick Press.
Facebook: HeWhoSuffers

Spirit Board Confessions
by Angela Zimmerman

"Just say it."

"It's not that easy," was his reply

Erica wondered if it ever would be. She drummed her fingers while she waited for an explanation. But like always, he was silent. She began to move her hands in circles, waiting for something to change. It was a nervous habit that she couldn't break.

Finally, he started talking.

"It's hard to say because you put me here. You put the bullet in me that sent me to Hell. If it weren't for you, I wouldn't have to talk this way. So, saying it ain't easy. But...I love you."

Angela Zimmerman is a writer living in the Southern United States. She has been published in Unnerving Magazine and Coffin Bell. You can find her personal writings at Conjure and Coffee.
Website: conjureandcoffee.com

Not Like the Movies
by Trisha Ridinger McKee

Rosie blinked at his pasty complexion, the foreboding black of his eyes. This was not like in the movies. He was not glowing. Still, she longed for that passion and the romance of being forever young with a boy as misunderstood as she was. She craved that passion. Most of all, she yearned to be loved.

But as he sank those yellow fangs into her neck, she squirmed. Alarm, not euphoria, charged through her veins. And just when she expected that immortality to grip her, he continued sucking. As her life drained out, she realised this was not the movies.

Trisha Ridinger McKee resides in a small town in Pennsylvania where love has proven to be a problem. Her work has appeared or is forthcoming in publications such as Tablet Magazine, The Oddville Press, Crab Fat Literary Magazine, Night to Dawn Magazine, Deep Fried Horror, 4 Star Stories, and more.

That Sibling Bond
by Nicole Little

My baby sister needed a kidney. A nurse myself, I'd seen too many people suffer needlessly due to a lack of organ donors. I was watching Maisie waste away before my very eyes. Torture.

After a year, she was at the top of the transplant list. The next kidney was hers. But these things take time. We were desperate and the clock was ticking.

So, it was up to me. I accessed the hospital records. I found a match. And now, as I stand outside his apartment, knife in my hand: I'm at peace with my decision.

Love you, sis.

Nicole Little is an award winning short story writer living in St. John's, Newfoundland, Canada. Her publishing credits include Sweet Sixteen (Kit Sora: The Artobiography, 2019), The Market and Last One Standing (Dystopia from the Rock, 2019); Far Out and On a Wing and a Prayer (Flights from the Rock, 2019). Her short story Doxxed placed favorably in the Writers Alliance of Newfoundland and Labrador's "A Nightmare on Water Street: Scary Story Reading". In her spare time, Nicole can be found with either a pen in her hand or her nose in a book. She is married with two daughters.

For Now Until Forever
by Michelle River

Poised on one knee with a princess cut diamond ring clutched in my hand, I waited anxiously for her response. I could sense her parents behind me, their fixed gaze burning a hole in the back of my head.

Her eyes sparkled like the diamond I had just ripped off her mother's cold fingers, her smile mirroring the same exact expression I had painstakingly sewn onto their faces just hours ago.

"Yes!" She launched herself towards me, embracing me in a hug as she showered me in kisses.

"For now until forever, just you and me."

"For now until forever."

Michelle River hails from Ontario, Canada where she is lives with her wonderful husband and fearless daughter. A lover of hot black coffee and everything dark and terrifying, she spends her nights writing horror and dreaming about all things that go bump in the night. For fun she writes short horror stories on reddit under the user name Drywitdrywine.
Facebook: MichelleRiverAuthor
Amazon: www.amazon.com/-/e/B07WKKB3Z5

Heartbroken
by D.J. Elton

Celina has golden skin, long tresses of wavy bronze hair that drifts behind her as she swims deep, deep below the surface of the siren seas.

She is sad. Wistful. Her heart is pining and starting to break. There is a man, a mortal to whom she has become an object of adoration.

This affection urges them to meet secretly in a dusty cave where octopi dwell, guarding its jagged walls.

Celina allows the mortal to touch her body, kiss her face, run his hands through her hair. Hold her cold green tail.

In breaking the law, she eternally suffers.

D.J. Elton is a writer living in Melbourne's west. As a child she came from England to Australia, on the last boat down the Suez Canal, where she underwent a sacrificial dunking ritual in the court of King Neptune, and has never looked back. She likes creating speculative micro fiction and short stories, as well as random essays. Her work has been published in several anthologies, and she has written a historical fantasy novella, 'The Merlin Girl.' When not playing with a pen, she likes most of all to go to the green country.

Cuddle Me Warm
by Catherine Kenwell

"Baby, I'm c-c-cold."

"I know, sweetheart. There's not much more I can do."

We'd managed to clamber out of the wreck before it burst into flames; thankfully, the heat kept us warm for the first night. But so many nights had passed since then.

"Are we ever going to be rescued, baby?"

"We're too weak to climb the cliff to the highway…I'm sorry. I'd do anything to save you, my love."

"Just hold me and keep me warm. I love you."

"I love you too, darling. But I'm afraid it's too late. You can't warm up by cuddling a corpse."

Catherine Kenwell is a Barrie, Ontario, mediator and author. After 30 successful years in corporate communications, she sustained a brain injury, lost her job, and joined the circus. She writes both horror/dark fiction and inspirational non-fiction. Her works have been published in Chicken Soup for the Soul, Trembling with Fear, Siren's Call, and HellBound Books. Website: www.catherinekenwell.com

From Afar
by A.R. Dean

Each day, I leave a token on her desk or at her home. From the first smile when we met, I knew she was my forever.

I can't understand why she's frightened by my gifts. She's complaining to anyone who will listen. She'll never figure out it's me, but I'm confused, I thought women loved romantic gestures.

Today is our anniversary. Tonight, I will sweep her away to the room I built just for her.

I sneak behind and knock her out. I'm thrilled to feel her weight in my arms. Before she wakes, I chain her up and wait.

A.R. Dean is a dark and twisted soul. Dean has spent their whole life spreading fear with the tales from their head. Best known for stories that terrify and show the evilest side of human nature. So, look for Dean haunting your local cemetery or under your bed, because they're here to spread the fear. Turn off your lights and enjoy a scare. Dean is being published in Black Hare Press's Beyond and Unravel Anthologies. Keep a lookout for more stories.
Facebook: A.R. Dean Author & Ghoul

Forever Autumn
by Frances Tate

I'm sure the aches every time I see you are psychosomatic. Regret weights my breathing, makes healed ribs twinge where you drove a post-coital stake through them, grazed my infatuated heart. Broke it. Metaphorically.

Fear, prejudice poisoned you.

Killed your love for the woman who will love you forever.

I lift emerald velvet from the carved box, insert this year's choice; ruby; the shade of wet maple leaves—and the lipstick I leave on your skull before closing the lid.

I open the ornate chest containing your heart. It's mine now; a gift in perpetuity. One promise you *will* keep.

Frances Tate is a British self-published writer of vampires and drabbles who lives in the north west of England. She enjoys gardening, exploring historical sites, cinema, reading and travelling. She's taken pleasure in flight-planning a cabbage white butterfly approach to careers, preferring to generalise rather than specialise. She trained as an Economics high school teacher and has a private pilot's licence amongst other things. Currently she writes (very restrained) overhaul instructions for an engineering company.

Her Smell Has Faded
by Stephen Herczeg

I didn't make it back into Bosnia until after well after curfew.

I wanted to get back to Nadia. The last few months together had been wonderful. Only duty forced me away.

The hotel stank of sweat and cigarettes.

Our room was empty. She'd left her scarf on the bed, still full of her perfume.

The next morning, as I visited a doctor about a story I was working, he brought me to the morgue.

She was there. Eyes closed. Half her head missing. I wept openly.

Now, all that is left is her scarf.

Even her smell has faded.

Stephen Herczeg is an IT Geek based in Canberra Australia. He has been writing for over twenty years and has completed a couple of dodgy novels, sixteen feature length screenplays and numerous short stories and scripts. His horror work has featured in Sproutlings, Hells Bells, Below the Stairs, Trickster's Treats #1 and #2, Shades of Santa, Behind the Mask, Beyond the Infinite; The Body Horror Book, Anemone Enemy, Petrified Punks and Beginnings. He has also had numerous Sherlock Holmes stories published through the Belanger Books - Sherlock Holmes anthologies.
Amazon: amazon.com/-/e/B07916SQQS
Facebook: stephenherczegauthor

What's Wrong?
by Stephen Herczeg

People ask, "What's wrong with me?"

I say, I don't know, but if I wait, my family will surely tell me.

That's all they ever seem to do.

It's always, don't do that. Don't do this. Don't say that. Don't say this. It's never ending.

But I fixed it.

I reckon I did the right thing. Finally, there were no complaints. Well, not after I tidied up the mess, anyway.

They just sit quietly. No grumbles. No moans. Nothing.

I think they are happier this way.

I really do love them. I always will, but they are beginning to smell.

Stephen Herczeg is an IT Geek based in Canberra Australia. He has been writing for over twenty years and has completed a couple of dodgy novels, sixteen feature length screenplays and numerous short stories and scripts. His horror work has featured in Sproutlings, Hells Bells, Below the Stairs, Trickster's Treats #1 and #2, Shades of Santa, Behind the Mask, Beyond the Infinite; The Body Horror Book, Anemone Enemy, Petrified Punks and Beginnings. He has also had numerous Sherlock Holmes stories published through the Belanger Books - Sherlock Holmes anthologies.
Amazon: amazon.com/-/e/B07916SQQS
Facebook: stephenherczegauthor

A Mother's Responsibility
by Radar DeBoard

Sylvia loved her children more than anything in the world. She would do anything to protect them. There were certain things that a mother must do for her children. A mother had responsibilities. Which was why she was up so late at night waiting for food.

Sylvia felt some movement and looked to see a man flailing about in her web. She descended quickly down the strands towards the screaming human. Her fangs sank into the man's neck, injecting her venom. After he stopped struggling, she wrapped him up. She moved up the web, with her children's dinner in tow.

Radar DeBoard is a horror movie and novel enthusiast who resides in the small town of Goddard, Kansas. He occasionally dabbles in writing, and enjoys to make dark tales for people to enjoy. He has had drabbles and short stories published in various electronic magazines and anthologies.
Facebook: WriterRadarDeBoard

Love is Blinded
by Shawn M. Klimek

Connie beamed lovingly at Zachary but saw him only in her mind's eye. The blast which had incinerated her stalker on that night of terror, so long ago, had also taken her sight. It had taken years for her to recover enough courage to meet another man. Full of lonesome self-pity, she had wondered, "Who could ever love a blind woman?"

But Zachary's gentleness and patience had gradually won her over. When he kissed her hand, her heart opened, and she longed to caress his face. "Not my face, please," he had protested. "The burn scars have made me ugly."

Shawn M. Klimek is the middle child of seven creative siblings, a globetrotting, U.S. military spouse, an internationally best-selling short-story writer, award-winning poet, and butler to a Maltese. More than one hundred and fifty of his stories and poems have been published in digital magazines or anthologies, including BHP's Deep Space, Eerie Christmas and every book so far in the Dark Drabbles series.
Website: jotinthedark.blogspot.com
Facebook: shawnmklimekauthor

Jonah's Delight
by Stuart Conover

Jonah and Jennifer were destined to be.

That was the deal he struck by the old oak tree.

Making a deal with that wonderful old witch

Now they'd live together without a hitch.

He'd always loved Jennifer's wit, poise, and grace.

But froze up inside when he looked at her face.

He couldn't form words to win her affection.

Even though she had always processed his attention.

Jonah knew they were destined to be together

Now to be married, she'd be with him forever.

Till death do them part would be written in stone.

Jonah would never again be alone.

Stuart Conover is a father, husband, rescue dog owner, published author, blogger, journalist, horror enthusiast, comic book geek, science fiction junkie, and IT professional. With all of that to cram in daily, we have no idea if or when he sleeps or how he gets writing done! (We suspect it has to do with having evil clones.) Stuart is a Chicago native and runs the author resource Horror Tree.

Earth to Mars, With Love
by C.L. Steele

She loved him. A love as simple as the alphabet and as complex as language. Their messages flew across space and time glimmering in white light across an otherwise dark screen. A's through Z's whispering love while never saying it. On Earth or Mars, he was her only need. The words were sometimes harsh, sometimes tender, mostly understanding. In his truth, he supported her life. Emotional words moved hurt to joy—all covered in deep longing. They created a world of their own, a planet wasn't needed. Through water-glistened eyes, bound forever to space, she knew she loved him, too.

C.L. Steele creates new worlds and mystical places filled with complex characters on exciting journeys. Her typical genre is Sci-Fi/Fantasy, where she concentrates on writing in the sub-genres of Magical Realism, Near Future, and Futuristic worlds. Published in numerous anthologies, she looks forward to the release of her debut novel. In the interim, she works on other novels and continues to write short stories, novellas, and poetry. She is featured as one of five international authors in ICWG Magazine through Clarendon Publishing House and is a contributing author to Blood Puddles Literary Journal.
Facebook: author.CLSteele
Instagram: @clsteele.author

Night Bus
by Dale Parnell

11.45pm, the last bus of the night. I know all the drivers and regular passengers. And then there's you. We've never spoken, but I love you.

Most nights you read. I often steal a glance at the cover so I can look it up online. Maybe I could start a conversation with you about what books you like to read? I never do.

I've started getting off the bus at your stop. If I could just talk to you, I know it would be okay.

You get on the bus with a policeman tonight and I smile. You've noticed me.

Dale Parnell lives in Staffordshire, England, with his wife and their imaginary dog, Moriarty. He has self-published two collections of short stories, "The Green Cathedral" and "Bramble and other stories". Dale also writes poetry, and is lucky enough to have pieces featured in several poetry and fiction anthologies.
Facebook: shortfictionauthor

Unrequited
by Erica Schaef

I stare up at Cupid. The winged cherub has adorned the ceiling of the city theatre for a hundred years, maybe longer. Only recently, though, have I felt the ache of his arrow. It's lodged securely in my chest like a long, twisted blade, splitting the ribcage and piercing the heart.

She is Lady Macbeth tonight. Her amber eyes are expressive, luminous orbs under the stage lights.

I can't look away from her. At the end of the performance, I drift down to her dressing room, and pass through the door. I wail for her, unheard, my wretched ghost song.

Erica Schaef worked as a Registered Nurse for many years before becoming a stay-at-home parent. Her short stories have been featured most recently by: Visual Verse (Vol. 06- Chapter 09), Blood Moon Rising Magazine (Issue 77), and HellBound Books ("The Toilet Zone"). More of her short stories will be in featured in upcoming anthologies by Fantasia Divinity ("Isolation"), and Jitter Press (Issue 8), as well as in the forthcoming issue of Still Point Arts Quarterly. She lives in rural Tennessee with her husband and two children.

The Perfect Neighbourhood
by Neen Cohen

"I love you, baby."

Billy leaned forward and kissed Jo.

On the ground between them Betty, gurgled from her bubbling cut throat.

"I love you too."

In the morning they would hear the news and be dutifully shocked.

They hoped the next neighbours remembered to pick up their dog's business during walks.

It was the only way to keep their lovely neighbourhood perfect.

Betty finally stopped making those dreadful noises. The dog had been far more considerate.

Jo and Billy continued on their evening stroll, hands entwined with each other's, while Billy hummed.

"I love living here."

"Living the dream."

Neen Cohen lives in Brisbane with her partner, son and fur babies. She is a writer of LGBTQI, dark fantasy and horror short stories and has a Bachelor of Creative Industries from QUT. She can often be found writing while sitting against a tombstone or tree in any number of graveyards.
Website: wordbubblessite.wordpress.com/
Facebook: neen.cohen.82

We Had Time for One Drink
by John Possidente

I had coffee ready when she woke up. I wanted to be nice, but not awkward nice or creepy. You never know how someone's going to be the next morning. I'd also piled her stuff—purse, little cooler with morbid stickers, shoes, jacket—neatly on a chair, not too near the door.

She stumbled out wearing my shirt, her face ashen. Uh-oh. Was she married?

Tiny, tiny voice: "Hold me?"

I did. She felt wooden, just stared over my shoulder at the chair with her things.

"What?" I asked. She pointed at the cooler.

"I forgot to deliver the kidney."

John Possidente enjoys coffee in the winter and raising monarch butterflies in the summer. He hopes to be an up-and-coming new writer someday.

The 13th Floor
by Ronnie Scissom

"Witch… I mean which floor, Ma'am," a handsome young businessman asks.

"13 please," a scantily clad woman in black replies.

"You smell nice," he awkwardly says.

"Thanks, it's a love spell," she replies.

The man looks at the elevator panel and he doesn't see a 13.

"Hold the 1 and the 3 buttons," the woman says.

He does as she says, and the blue 1 and 3 buttons turn red.

The elevator stops, and the door opens to a room of terrifying creatures having a rave. The Devil himself is the DJ.

"Come along, lover," the witch says.

He follows.

Ronnie Scissom hails from Gruetli-Laager. When not working or writing, he likes to explore the beauty of the Cumberland Plateau. He dabbles in acting and has had background roles in several hit television series and motion pictures.

Surrounded
by V. Mylynne Smith

A cluster of cops stood between me and the woman I loved. Mowing them down wasn't easy, but I did it for her. When I reached her, I was out of ammo and bleeding. She wrapped her arms around my neck and kissed me.

The metal cuffs on her wrists rubbed against my skin as she held me. The building was surrounded by officers with their weapons drawn. We knew this would be our last embrace.

Putting my hands on her hips, we waltzed as they broke through the barricaded doors. I felt the bullets, but I only saw her.

V. Mylynne Smith primarily writes thrillers, but sometimes dips a toe into horror. Her love of psychology helps her craft malicious characters with the worst intentions. She aims to create twists and turns that keep the reader guessing until the end. Smith is an Oklahoman that moved to Northwest Arkansas after meeting her husband. The pair live together in a cozy house with two pets: a pitbull named Renegade and a feisty cat named Bandit. When Smith isn't stringing words together, you can find her in front of a mirror with make-up in hand or baking something delicious and fattening.

Forever Yours
by D.M. Burdett

He thrusts and grunts; his weekly treat.

But I only feel the wind teasing my hair, and the warm sunshine on my face, as I listen to the trees whispering his name.

I watch from cloudy eyes as he finishes and then collapses against me, his hot breath against my cheek.

When his loving heart is steady, he pulls up his pants.

"You'll always be my girl," he says as he caresses my bone-white cheek, presses a wet kiss to my bloated lips.

Then he pushes my body back into the shallow grave and tenderly re-covers my swollen, black flesh.

First published in *Forest of Fear*, 2019

__D.M. Burdett__ initially roamed as an army brat, but now lives in Australia where she spends her days avoiding drop bears and killer spiders. She has published a Sci-Fi series, has short stories in various anthologies, and has published two children's series. She is currently working on the first book in a dystopian series.
Website: www.dmburdett.com
Facebook: DMBurdett

Sacrifice
by Jo Mularczyk

"But Astrid, you love flying."

"I know what I'm giving up, Cora," Astrid said with a reassuring smile. "He's worth it."

"It will be painful. Agonising. I've only seen a separation performed once, but the memory never left me."

"I'm ready. Please do it. The waiting is...AAAARGH!" She dropped to her knees amidst the tattered remains of her wings. The pain faded, replaced by jubilation. She could now walk the earth beside her beloved.

An anguished cry rent the air, "Astrid, what have you done?"

She turned to see the impossible—he stood before her as an angel.

Jo Mularczyk's stories and poems appear in magazines and anthologies including - The School Magazine's Blast Off and Touchdown; Zinewest 2017, 2018, 2019; Short and Twisted 2017; Open House 2 and 3; Short Tales 4 and 5; Christmas Tales 4; Wonderment; an upcoming Bloomsbury UK book of poems for children; fourW thirty; and several upcoming publications. Jo mentors gifted and talented students' writing groups, runs junior writing workshops and is a co-author with the student literacy program, Littlescribe. Through Littlescribe Jo provides writing tips and story starters for students to complete as co-authors. Jo lives in Australia with her husband and three children.
Website: www.jomularczyk.com
Facebook: jo.mularczyk.author

I Know He's There
by Stephen Herczeg

It was horrible, but it was just an accident.

I was running late, again. Got my pants on, grabbed my jacket as I ran for the stairs.

Jimbo ran alongside me. He's a good dog. So loyal. So affectionate. Always with me.

That day he was too close.

I tripped over him as I hit the stairs. Bounced down them. Crack.

Now I'm down deep in the ground. It's quiet and dark.

I can feel soft feet on the grass above. I know he's there. Lying. Waiting.

I just want to cuddle and pat him.

He's a such good dog.

Stephen Herczeg is an IT Geek based in Canberra Australia. He has been writing for over twenty years and has completed a couple of dodgy novels, sixteen feature length screenplays and numerous short stories and scripts. His horror work has featured in Sproutlings, Hells Bells, Below the Stairs, Trickster's Treats #1 and #2, Shades of Santa, Behind the Mask, Beyond the Infinite; The Body Horror Book, Anemone Enemy, Petrified Punks and Beginnings. He has also had numerous Sherlock Holmes stories published through the Belanger Books - Sherlock Holmes anthologies.
Amazon: amazon.com/-/e/B07916SQQS
Facebook: stephenherczegauthor

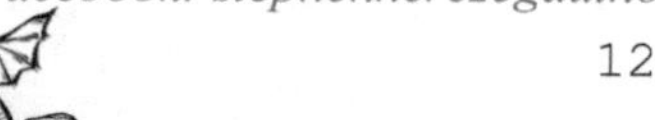

1962
by David Bowmore

The whole world loves her. And I love her, too.

Everyone loves her—except perhaps the movie studios.

She has episodes of, shall we say, weakness.

If it weren't for our high profiles, we would never have been introduced. If it weren't for our high profiles, we might be happy together.

However, she threatens to talk, to tell the world of our love.

Plans were already afoot when she sang Happy Birthday.

A gangster has everything arranged. Hoover has made sure no one talks.

She's special, the public will always love her.

But it's more important that Americans love me.

David Bowmore has lived here, there and everywhere, but now lives in Yorkshire with his wonderful wife and a small white poodle. He has worn many hats in his time; head chef, teacher and landscape gardener. His first collection of short stories 'The Magic of Deben Market' is available from Clarendon House.
Website: davidbowmore.co.uk
Facebook: davidbowmoreauthor

An Unfinished Story
by Nerisha Kemraj

Why do I still see you, even when I don't want to?

Yours was a love I was not ready to receive,

and now it lingers,

not knowing whether to stay or to leave...

My eyes wander

through every intersection

hoping to find you,

My mind never sleeps,

always awake to remind me

of you.

Why do you still haunt me?

A presence I try to ignore.

Why do you still taunt me?

I can't take this anymore.

My dreams follow you

into each waking moment,

to an empty room

echoing my heart...

Reminding me,

of what

we never were.

Nerisha Kemraj resides in Durban, South Africa with her husband and two mischievous daughters. Writing since 2017, she has had over 100 short stories and poems published in various publications, both print and online. She has also received an Honourable Mention Award for her tanka in the Fujisan Taisho 2019 Tanka Contest. She holds a Bachelor's degree in Communication Science, and a Post Graduate Certificate in Education from University of South Africa.
Amazon: amazon.com/author/nerisha_kemraj
Facebook: Nerishakemrajwriter

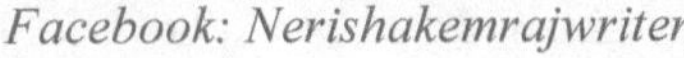

Stay
by J.W. Garrett

Sam followed his ex to her place. *One drink then, gone.*

The room… A warning went off in his head. The music, the lighting…

"Listen, I can't stay. One drink."

"And here it is." Jasmine lifted her glass to his. He tossed the liquid back in one gulp, then kissed her cheek.

"Wait. Stay. Just a few minutes."

His eyes blurred. He stumbled.

Waking to concrete underneath him and grating clatter, he stared ahead to a wall closing him in, brick by brick.

His limbs hung, useless. Words wouldn't form.

Another brick lowered, sealing him in.

"Stay. You promised me."

J.W. Garrett has been writing in one form or another since she was a teenager. She currently lives in Florida with her family but loves the mountains of Virginia where she was born. Her writings include YA fantasy as well as short stories. Since completing Remeon's Quest-Earth Year 1930, the prequel in her YA fantasy series, Realms of Chaos, she has been hard at work on the next in the series, scheduled to release August 2020. When she's not hanging out with her characters, her favourite activities are reading, running and spending time with family.
Website: www.jwgarrett.com
BHC Press: www.bhcpress.com/Author_JW_Garrett.html

Love Letters
by Terri A. Arnold

Her dog Max is curled up on the rug at the bottom of the bed. He gives me a disinterested glance as I give his head a gentle rub and he closes his eyes.

I step to the head of her bed and inhale deeply, savouring the scent of her perfume as I place the note I've written for her on her pillow. I can't wait to see the look on her face when she realises how much I adore her.

Headlights shine in through her window, and I hurry into the closet. It's time to hide for a while.

***Terri A. Arnold** is an avid reader turned writer from a small town in Nova Scotia, who has spent her life reading and wishing she was writing. Although she has written a lot in those years, she has only recently begun to submit pieces for publication. With ongoing encouragement from family and writing challenges with friends, Arnold felt the urge to try her hand at publishing.*

Won't Let You Go
by Matthew Wallace

The incantations were read, and the ritual was complete. Now, all he had to do was wait. She looked so beautiful. He wasn't sure how he had gone three days without her.

When the police said that she was dead, he hadn't believed them; wouldn't accept that a drunk driver had taken her. Then, when his worst fears were confirmed, he refused to let her go.

He stood in the morgue, ready to bring her back.

She shook as the dark magic took hold of her.

"Baby?" he whispered, elated.

She howled, pouncing and sinking her teeth into his flesh.

Matthew Wallace is a published short fiction author and an aspiring novelist. He currently lives in Houston, Tx with his wife and attended the University of Houston for Psychology. In addition to writing, he has performed stand-up comedy all across the United States of America.

Orpheus
by Mia Ram

What is the duty of a husband? To love, to cherish, to protect. I do much of the latter for Lydia. I see the fear in those wide, azure eyes at every knock on our door.

Don't let them take me back, she pleads. *I can't go back.*

And so I lie for Lydia. I tell the officers, her family, the neighbours, that I know nothing. I keep her safe by my side. They'll never know it was I who rescued her from the damp earth and brought her home where she belongs.

Only I see the life in her.

Mia Ram is an emerging writer from Huntersville, North Carolina. She writes fantasy, science fiction, and horror fiction, and has previously had her work adapted for the No Sleep podcast.

Eternal Love
by Owen Morgan

How does one thwart the Grim Reaper and keep his skeletal grasp away from a loved one? It's simple; one gives him a substitute.

I've never spoken with the foul overseer of death, but I have kept my dear Nancy safe from him. She's so sweet and kind. Why would anyone wish her dead? If I keep offering sacrifices which resemble my beloved, then why would he take her?

I've tried to be merciful in my quest: the most subtle poisons on the elderly, insane, and those who wish to shed their insufferable mortal coil. I do it for love.

Owen Morgan writes science fiction, fantasy, and alternate history, and lives in the fishing port of Steveston, British Columbia.
Website: httpwwwkingauthor.wordpress.com
Twitter: @owen_morgan1066

I'm Sorry
by Ken "Timber" Halhober

Caitlin lay in bed and cried. Tom left in a huff after a discussion of who loved who the most. He said he would kill everyone in the neighbourhood to prove it, and she didn't believe him. That was three hours ago, and she had been crying since.

Little rocks tapping the bedroom window caught her attention, and she rushed over. Opening the window, she gasped, seeing Tom next to the bodies of those in their neighbourhood. Their bodies, mutilated and broken, spelling out the words "I LOVE YOU" in big letters. She would never doubt his love ever again.

Ken "Timber" Halhober *has been writing most of his life, mainly screenplays but has been delving more into stories as he goes. Always trying to improve as he goes.*

Love Lives
by Ronnie Scissom

"Welcome home sweetheart," a guy says as he holds a door open.

A woman in a torn and bloodstained dress enters.

"I fixed you a place to rest downstairs," he says.

The woman's bloodshot eyes stay fixed on him.

"Rrrr," she says.

"Great job, Piper. That's right, I'm Ryan," he replies.

Ryan sits on the couch. Piper walks over and stands in front of him.

"Oh, look! The hospital forgot to take this off," Ryan says as he removes a toe tag from Piper's foot.

"I love you," Ryan says as he leans in for a kiss.

She bites him.

Ronnie Scissom hails from Gruetli-Laager. When not working or writing, he likes to explore the beauty of the Cumberland Plateau. He dabbles in acting and has had background roles in several hit television series and motion pictures.

The Perfect Ring
by G. Allen Wilbanks

"What about this one?" I asked, holding up a two-carat diamond in a platinum setting.

"Pretty," she agreed. "But I don't like the princess cut. What else do they have?"

I put the ring back into its velvet holder.

"I want you to have the perfect engagement ring," I assured her, "but we're running out of time. You need to make a decision soon, my love."

I moved the body of the store manager out of the way, unfortunately getting more blood on my clothing. Reaching into the broken display case, I plucked out another ring.

"What about this one?"

G. Allen Wilbanks is a member of the Horror Writers Association (HWA) and has published over 100 short stories in various magazines and on-line venues. He is the author of two short story collections, and the novel, When Darkness Comes. Website: www.gallenwilbanks.com Blog: DeepDarkThoughts.com

Dead Stare
by Terry Miller

Unrequited love is the worst kind of love. Scooter Lyles was a man of defeated hopes. Tonya Williams had his eye since the fourth grade. Now they were adults, rarely seeing one another in passing.

Scooter was a grease monkey, hardly someone Tonya would bat a lash at. Her car was in the shop. He'd hide in the trunk when she picked her car up that evening.

Scooter shut the trunk, the evening sun peering through the cracks. He turned to see another pair of eyes looking at him, locked in a dead stare. The car's engine roared to life.

Terry Miller lives in Portsmouth, Ohio. His work has been featured in Sanitarium Magazine, Devolution Z, Jitter, Rhysling Anthology 2017, Poetry Quarterly, Sirens Call Ezine, The Horror Tree's Trembling With Fear, SpillWords, Organic Ink Vol. I, Curses & Cauldrons Anthology from Blood Song Books, Forest of Fear from Blood Song Books, the Dark Drabble Anthology Series from Black Hare Press, 100 Word Zombie Bites from Reanimated Writers Press, Scary Snippets, Guilty Pleasures & Other Dark Delights, 100 Word Horrors 3, and O Unholy Night In Deathlehem from Grinning Skull Press.
Facebook: tmiller2015
Amazon: amazon.com/author/millerterryl

For Catherine
by Jason Holden

You looked so sad when I died. How could I not make the deal?

Two years in hell; for each one, you live a happy life.

They strip my flesh, burn my eyes. Each day is a fresh agony.

From time to time they show me images of you, with your new love.

You smile at him the way you used to smile at me.

It's meant to torment me, make me regret my decision and break my spirit.

It does not.

If the Devil offered me that deal again today, I would take it.

Just to see you smile.

Jason Holden is a human. He lives here and there in the UK, always with his wife, daughter and fur baby. His primary goal is to raise his daughter to adulthood without any major damage. When he can, he writes. He thinks he does it well, but you can be the judge of that. He has been published in a few anthologies here and there, has been praised and put down for his writing. You can find and follow him on Facebook, although he asks you only follow him on Facebook and not through the streets. That's just creepy.
Facebook: Jason Holden-Author

Chained
by Rowanne S. Carberry

I know I'm awake. My eyes are open. All I see is black.

Trying to move my body, I start with my hands. A feeling of cold metal pressing against my wrists greets me.

"You're awake, good."

The voice sends shivers down my spine. I know who it is.

I start to struggle.

"Don't Hannah. I don't want to hurt you," he whispers.

A snort of laughter escapes me.

"Take these off me then," I tell him, rattling the handcuffs.

His hand strokes my face, I try not to flinch.

"I love you," followed by a key in the cuffs.

Rowanne S. Carberry *was born in England in 1990, where she stills lives now with her cat Wolverine. Rowanne has always loved writing, and her first poem was published at the age of 15, but her ambition has always been to help people. Rowanne studied at the University of Sunderland where she completed combined honours of Psychology with Drama. Rowanne writes to offer others an escape. Although Rowanne writes in varied genres each story or poem she writes will often have a darkness to it, which helped coin her brand, Poisoned Quill Writing – Wicked words from a poisoned quill.*
Facebook: PoisonedQuillWriting
Instagram: @poisoned_quill_writing

Devotion
by Kaitlyn Arnett

"You know I'd do anything for you," he told her one morning when it was bitter and cold, his hands stained a delicate crimson.

She never responded, but he smiled anyway. After all, his darling always had been outspoken.

When the moon was high and the stars danced, he promised her, "I'd burn the world if that was what you wanted." His hands were painted scarlet, dipped in ill intentions.

She remained silent, still in her ancient grave. She'd never respond, and never had. And even so, he promised her his world, his everything.

After all, he was in love.

Kaitlyn Arnett is a teen author who has been writing for five years. She focuses on the fantasy and thriller genres, specifically drabbles and short stories.

Dying for Love
by J.M. Meyer

I'm outside Dunkin' Donuts, the spurned engagement ring in my pocket.

Joni ended our engagement and said we're through. But that girl meant nothing. I was drunk!

We're meeting to exchange apartment keys.

Joni has to realise how meaningless her life would be without me. That's why I hired a crew to stage an accident.

When the director yells "Action!" Joni is parked nearby. Her mouth agape, Joni sees: overturned cars, screaming actors, her bloodied dead boyfriend. She looks sad before the truck slams into her as she is running to me. At least I know she cares. Did care.

J.M. Meyer is a writer, artist and small business owner living in New York, where she received her master's degree from Teachers College, Columbia University. Jacqueline enjoys writing speculative fiction and mysteries. Her favorite author is Alice Munro and her favorite film…is…anything horror related. Jacqueline also enjoys hiking with her dog Molly and the company of her husband Bruce and daughters; Julia, Emma and Lauren. Jacqueline's Mantra lately; there's no such thing as failing, it's called learning.
Website: jmoranmeyer.net
Amazon: www.amazon.com/author/jacquelinemoranmeyer

The Perfect Gift
by Stuart Conover

Kristen knew she had to get something for the love of her life.

But what to get Kevin?

What did you get for the man who had it all?

Kevin had money, toys, and, turning red thinking about it, the perfect woman.

What would make him happy?

She knew he always wanted to move forward.

So, at long last, she figured it out.

The gift took longer than expected to prepare.

Kristen delivered the present in person.

Answering the door, he looked confused but took the gift.

She insisted he open it.

Immediately.

Inside?

The head of his perfect girlfriend.

Stuart Conover is a father, husband, rescue dog owner, published author, blogger, journalist, horror enthusiast, comic book geek, science fiction junkie, and IT professional. With all of that to cram in daily, we have no idea if or when he sleeps or how he gets writing done! (We suspect it has to do with having evil clones.) Stuart is a Chicago native and runs the author resource Horror Tree.

The Grand Pour
by Eddie D. Moore

Darren usually worked security during the night shift, but they needed extra hands to keep back the crowds and make sure that the delivery trucks were not delayed. The construction workers danced a predictable routine as over one-hundred million pounds of concrete was poured into the foundation.

A slow breath of relief slipped past Darren's lips as the sun broke through the cloudy sky. He counted forty-seven concrete trucks before losing count. When he heard his wife's ringtone, love filled his heart and he smiled.

"Hi, honey. There's nothing to worry about. They will never find any of those bodies."

Eddie D. Moore travels hundreds of hours a year, and he fills that time by listening to audiobooks. When he isn't playing with his grandchildren, he writes his own stories. You can find a list of his publications on his blog or by visiting his Amazon Author Page. While you're there, be sure to pick up a copy of his mini-anthology Misfits & Oddities.
Website: eddiedmoore.wordpress.com
Amazon: amazon.com/author/eddiedmoore

The Unethical Vegan
by Jacob Baugher

I hate the way humans taste. I'm vegan. But Gerald? He'll tear into a butt-cheek like a side of beef.

Fog rolls off Lake Erie; shrouds Cleveland in a misty coat. I'm supposed to be "hunting." I stop for a coffee instead. I gotta get away for a while. There's so much blood in our basement. Brains and intestines.

I hate him, but he takes care of me… I guess I "owe" him.

A fratboy steps out of line with his macchiato. His bro-tank reads: "U Good?"

Target acquired. I'm doing this for you, baby.

"Hi." I smile. "I'm Shawna."

Jacob Baugher teaches Creative Writing at a small university near Pittsburgh, PA. When he's not teaching or coaching the track team, he can be found in the Cuyahoga Valley hiking with his wife and son or brewing beer on his front porch. He's received honourable mentions for his work in the Writers of the Future contest and he co-edits a series of Fantasy and Science Fiction anthologies titled Continuum. His work also appears in Black Hare's Deep Space and Area-51 anthologies, as well as in the Dark Drabble Anthologies Worlds, Angels, Monsters, Beyond, and Unravel. He also hates pineapple on pizza.

Together Forever
by Ali House

Ella looked down at Liam's sleeping face and gently caressed his cheek. "I know you're thinking of leaving me," she whispered softly. "I know you think it won't work out between us, but you're wrong. We belong together, forever and ever, just like you said when we first met." She leaned in, kissing his lips.

Lying down, she took the mask from the doctor and held it over her face, breathing in the anaesthetic. Soon they would be together. Soon she would have Liam's heart stitched to hers, side by side within her chest, and they would never be apart.

Ali House is the author of sci-fi/fantasy novels *The Six Elemental* and *The Fifth Queen*, along with various short stories in the "From the Rock" series published by Engen Books. She is a traveller, baker, and fan of the Oxford comma. Website: engenbooks.com/tag/house-blog/

Butterflies
by Dale Parnell

When Matthew was nine, he collected butterflies. He found an old jam jar in his father's shed that smelled of turpentine, and although Matthew felt sad killing them, you couldn't appreciate their beauty until they had been carefully pinned to a board. At least they died peacefully, gently even.

Now twenty-six, Matthew is lost and alone. Women are so frustrating, always too busy to take the time to get to know him.

From the depths of his memory, Matthew remembers his butterflies. He thinks of the jam jar and smiles. A quiet, gentle death.

Isn't that what we all want?

Dale Parnell lives in Staffordshire, England, with his wife and their imaginary dog, Moriarty. He has self-published two collections of short stories, "The Green Cathedral" and "Bramble and other stories". Dale also writes poetry, and is lucky enough to have pieces featured in several poetry and fiction anthologies.
Facebook: shortfictionauthor

Let Me Recount the Ways
by John H. Dromey

He said…

I love each and everything about you, big and small, except for a few of your more annoying quirks.

For instance, the way you flirt with the wait staff in restaurants. Your snide remarks about my supposed lack of fashion sense. Your liking cats better than dogs. Your choice of friends. Just to name a few.

And, finally, what irritates the life out of me above everything else is your pretence of *naïveté* in serious situations.

Any questions?

She said…

Just a couple. Why are you down on one knee, and what's in that little box you're holding?

John H. Dromey was born in northeast Missouri, USA. He enjoys reading—mysteries in particular—and writing in a variety of genres. In addition to contributing to the Black Hare Press series of Dark Drabbles anthologies, he's had short fiction published in Alfred Hitchcock's Mystery Magazine, Martian Magazine, Mystery Weekly, Stupefying Stories Showcase, Thriller Magazine, Unfit Magazine, and elsewhere, as well as in numerous anthologies, including Chilling Horror Short Stories (Flame Tree Publishing, 2015).

Roommate Unrealised
by Peter J. Foote

Tyler peers through his spyhole and watches as Candice showers and dresses for work.

Dashing through her cluttered house hunting for her keys, Candice rubs Ziggi's ears before leaving for work.

The house silent, Tyler releases the attic hatch and climbs down the ladder to meet Ziggi waiting at the floor. "She forgot to feed you again, didn't she?" Tyler asks as the cat weaves between his feet.

"Let's get you breakfast. Do you think she'd notice if I spruced up some? This is getting out of control," Tyler asks the cat as he makes himself comfortable in Candice's house.

Peter J. Foote is a bestselling speculative fiction writer from Nova Scotia. Outside of writing, he runs a used bookstore specialising in fantasy & sci-fi, cosplays, and alternates between red wine and coffee as the mood demands. His short stories can be found in both print and in ebook form, with his story "Sea Monkeys" winning the inaugural "Engen Books/Kit Sora, Flash Fiction/Flash Photography" contest in March of 2018. As the founder of the group "Genre Writers of Atlantic Canada", Peter believes that the writing community is stronger when it works together.
Twitter: @PeterJFoote1
Website: peterjfooteauthor.wordpress.com

Nosferatu
by Jasmine Jarvis

Watching you for so long, night after night, has become too much for my ancient dead heart to bear, and my longing for you is overwhelming. You don't have any idea of who I am and what I am capable of, but please don't be scared. The moment you smiled at me in passing in the street last night, I knew you had finally seen me. I will come to you tonight, my love, my fangs sharp and embrace strong. You cannot fight me now. In the morning, they will find your corpse, and your blood will finally be mine.

Jasmine Jarvis is a teller of tales and scribbler of scribbles. She lives in Brisbane, Australia with her husband Michael, their two children, Tilly and Mish; Ripley, their German Shepherd, and indoor fat cat, Dwight K. Shrute.

True Love
by Nicole Little

"Hey, Élodie?" I whispered, her head next to mine, "I'm sorry I was gone for so long."

I'd heard the stories from my grandfather, of men off at war whose girlfriends had waited until they'd returned.

See, that's my idea of true love.

I just *knew* Élodie would be one of those girls. My heart ached each day I'd been away, but I needed to be certain. Then we'd be together.

I mean sure, she'd screamed for a while after I first let her out of the basement, but she was quiet now. And I would never leave her again.

Nicole Little is an award winning short story writer living in St. John's, Newfoundland, Canada. Her publishing credits include Sweet Sixteen (Kit Sora: The Artobiography, 2019), The Market and Last One Standing (Dystopia from the Rock, 2019); Far Out and On a Wing and a Prayer (Flights from the Rock, 2019). Her short story Doxxed placed favorably in the Writers Alliance of Newfoundland and Labrador's "A Nightmare on Water Street: Scary Story Reading". In her spare time, Nicole can be found with either a pen in her hand or her nose in a book. She is married with two daughters.

No Tomorrow
by Carole de Monclin

Today, in your arms, life is perfect.

But, one day, you'll die, and I'll be left behind.

One day, a doctor will tell us you have cancer, or the police will call to notify me of a terrible accident.

One day, you'll get Alzheimer's disease, and you'll forget about me.

One day, I'll find lipstick on your collar, and you'll leave me.

Whatever the future holds, it can only be tears, misery, and loneliness.

Today's so perfect.

Drink this, my love.

I can't stop time, but I can make sure tomorrow never comes, and all this pain never finds us.

Carole de Monclin travels both the real world and imaginary ones. She's lived in France, Australia, and the USA; visited 25+ countries; and explored Mars, Ceres, and many distant planets. She writes to invite people on a journey. Her stories can be found in The Arcanist, The Deep Space Anthology, and every volume of the Dark Drabbles series.
Website: CaroledeMonclin.com
Twitter: @CaroledeMonclin

No Obstacle Too Great
by Kimberly Rei

I peered through the old-fashioned telescope. The shop owner said dated back to the 1800s, but I knew it was older than that.

The first time I watched her, the scope spoke to me, whispering of my love.

She was with that cute girl from HR, but the scope told me what to do. I had a picture of them together. I carefully cut one piece away from the photo. Through the viewfinder, the blonde screamed as her leg vanished and she fell over.

A few more cuts and she would be out of the way. Out of my way.

Kimberly Rei has been writing for as long as she can remember. At five years old, her parents gifted her with a set of Children's Classics that she had no hope of reading. Yet. The potential alone sparked a love of words that has never wavered. Kim has taught writing workshops and edited novels for Authors You May Recognize. She has published several short stories and now can't stop chasing paper dragons. She currently lives in Tampa Bay, Florida with her wife and an abundance of gorgeous beaches to explore.

Pieces of You
by R.J. Greene

Finally. She's still.

"What do we take first?"

Wayne regarded the figure for a moment. Warm. Pliable. Pale.

"She's still breathing."

"That's okay. She'll keep for longer. Everyone says you have her eyes." He popped one out with his thumb. A soft squish.

Charlene held it near her face. "What do you think?"

"Doesn't really match."

"I always wanted her cheekbones."

He whipped out his pocket knife. With surgical precision, he excised the cheek flesh and laid it delicately on Charlene's face.

'Does the nose match?'

A slice, a tug. He held it up. "Yep. She's your mother all right."

R.J. Greene is a woman of a certain age, who simply loves to write. She's had a lot of different jobs, including caterer, dressmaker, and her first job, as a turn down girl for a hotel. Make of that what you will. After taking the scenic route through education, her current gig is teaching. Marking papers keeps her well supplied with fiction. She's lived on four continents, but loves London most.

Sam's Son
by James Lipson

"Honey, have you seen Sam?"

"He's outside. Would you please go talk to him, he's struggling again."

"Hey, buddy. You okay?"

"Yeah."

"Are you sure? You don't seem like everything is okay."

"It happened again…I popped another ball, the red one this time. I tried, Dad, I really did. I don't know what I did wrong. I was gentle like you said, I didn't push that hard."

"I know sweetheart, It's okay. It's not your fault, you're still learning—no one expects you to figure this out overnight. It's just a ball, Samson. We can get you another one."

James Lipson's debut book, *Fallen and Other Stories*, was published in 2019. His short stories have appeared in Black Hare Press Anthologies, Teleport Magazine, Inner Circle's Writers Group Anthologies, and others. With a background in art, James has naturally turned to illustrating as he writes, bringing many of his short stories to life not only with descriptive detail, but also detailed visual imagery.
Website: www.jameslipson.com
Instagram: jameslipsonart

It Takes Time
by G. Allen Wilbanks

She said she doesn't feel the same way I do, but that's okay. It takes time to get to know the real me. I am a patient man. I will give her all the time she needs. Once she realises what a kind, warm, wonderful person I am, she will love me just as much as I love her.

She does not believe that, yet. She insists she will never love me. Even when I give her extra food or a longer chain to move around, she still resists me.

She'll come around. It will just take a little time.

G. Allen Wilbanks is a member of the Horror Writers Association (HWA) and has published over 100 short stories in various magazines and on-line venues. He is the author of two short story collections, and the novel, When Darkness Comes. Website: www.gallenwilbanks.com
Blog: DeepDarkThoughts.com

Perfectly Matched
by Christopher T. Dabrowski
Translated by Julia Mraczny

We're like two halves of an apple. Perfectly matched. I know all her thoughts. I know the pleasures and perversions she enjoys. I know what kind of filth grows in her mind. I let her do the bad things that she always wanted to do but was afraid to do. I give it to her. So why does she hate me so much when we complement each other so perfectly? Why the damn exorcisms when we live in perfect symbiosis?

I have possessed so many women in my long life as a demon, and yet I still don't understand them.

Christopher T. Dabrowski was born in Poland in 1978 year. He has stories published in "Anomaly" (2019 - Royal Hawaiian Press), "Escape" (2019 - Royal Hawaiian Press), "Anomalia" (2019 - Royal Hawaiian Press), "La fuga" (2019 - Royal Hawaiian Press), "Deathbirth" (2008 - Armoryka), "Anima vilis" (2010 - Initium), "Grobbing" (2012 - Novae Res), "Deathbirth and other stories" (2012 & 2017 - Agharta & Armoryka), "Z życia Dr Abble" (2013 - Agharta), "Orgazmokalipsa" (2016 - Alternatywne), "Anomalia" (2016 - Forma), "Ucieczka" (2017 - Dom Horroru) & "Nie w inność" (2019 - Waspos), PLAYBOY
Facebook: Krzysztof-T-Dąbrowski-166581686751600

The Wages of Sin
by Shelly Jarvis

He says I'm in love with him. I didn't realise it until he told me so. Now I see he must be right. He is always right.

I learn at his feet, drink from the cup he gives, hang on each honeyed word. He is my everything. When he calls me to his room, I can barely contain my glee. I've been praying for this night.

I'm surprised by the other people in the room. I thought we'd ascend together, alone. But seven others rest nearby with frothing, wine-stained lips.

He says, "Ready?"

I smile. "Anything for you, Father Gregor."

***Shelly Jarvis** is a speculative fiction author from West Virginia, US. She found a life-long love of sci-fi and fantasy in the 3rd grade when she found Madeleine L'Engle's "A Wrinkle in Time." Shelly is an avid reader, a Whovian, the ideal viewer of dog rescue videos, and undoubtedly Ravenclaw. She currently has three YA sci-fi books available for purchase on Amazon. Website: www.ShellyJarvis.com*

Closed Door
by Nerisha Kemraj

Every second I long to say something

but I remember our last meeting

and how you preferred silence

above all else...

Chills run down my spine,

recalling the disdain

that emanated from the new you.

And I shudder,

shutting myself within the margins of my own insanity.

Agonising without clarity.

Unsure of why this tragedy

befell us

I pick up the phone to connect once again,

to rekindle our love.

But then I fall back,

remembering

how you turned away

when I tried to explain.

Your pain evident.

A permanent reminder;

the door to our world

has long since closed.

Nerisha Kemraj resides in Durban, South Africa with her husband and two mischievous daughters. Writing since 2017, she has had over 100 short stories and poems published in various publications, both print and online. She has also received an Honourable Mention Award for her tanka in the Fujisan Taisho 2019 Tanka Contest. She holds a Bachelor's degree in Communication Science, and a Post Graduate Certificate in Education from University of South Africa.
Amazon: amazon.com/author/nerisha_kemraj
Facebook: Nerishakemrajwriter

Letters from a Lover
by Destiny Eve Pifer

Letters fall from the ceiling as she stretches across the bed. In just a few short weeks, they had fallen madly in love.

A lover trapped behind metal doors, with only a glimpse of the sunlight. His crime had been murder, but she did not care. She loved him, needed him, desired him.

On the edge of town in that tiny cramped cell, he plotted his escape. Soon they would be together. He would kill anyone who stood in his way. Now, as the thunder boomed across the sky, he put forth his plan.

Tonight would be the night they met.

Destiny Eve Pifer is a published author whose work has appeared in numerous anthologies and magazines. Her stories have been featured in FATE Magazine, True Confessions, Spotlight on Recovery and Country Magazine. A lover of all things supernatural and spooky she resides in Punxsutawney, Pennsylvania with her son Dartanyan.

Love For You
by C.L. Williams

The love I have for you is real

I only want to tell you how I feel

Here I am in your closet, too afraid to speak

Because when I see you, I grow weak

If only I could tell you I love you

I know that you will love me too

Even if you don't know me

I know you will love what you see

I want to jump out and yell "Surprise!"

Then you will see the love in my eyes

I want to be your love, remove your pain

Until then, your closet is where I'll remain

C.L. Williams is an international best-selling author currently living in central Virginia. He has written eight poetry books, four novellas, one novel, and a contributor to a multitude of anthologies and magazines. His most recent anthology appearance ANGELS: Dark Drabbles #2 from Black Hare Press became a number one in hot new releases. C.L. Williams is currently working on his second novel and a new poetry book.
Facebook: writer434
Twitter: @writer_434

Good Riddance
by Cassandra Angler

The sight of you makes my heart hammer against my chest. The way your strong hands turn the steering wheel, the whiteness of the teeth in your smile. Eyes black as night, scanning our surroundings as you drag her body from the backseat. The car stinks of her, but I am glad she's gone. Good riddance. I watch as you tug the rings from her finger and cover her in leaves. I hold my hand flat as you get back in the car. You slide the rings into their rightful place. "Let her rot, Baby. I'll be your wife now."

Cassandra Angler *is a married mother of four who lives in the State of Ohio in the USA. When she isn't busy caring for her family, Cassandra works on her upcoming novel due out in November of 2020 titled Contaminated. Cassandra has three short story publications as well as several flash fiction and drabble publications.*

Mythical Proportions
by John H. Dromey

The bulk of a centaur's body was concealed by a hedgerow as he paid court to a fair lady in an ivory tower. He was reduced to extolling his strong points verbally.

"I've never been unseated in a joust. I can defend your honour in a trial by combat."

"It's too late for that. Besides, I'm a pacifist."

"I have two left feet when it comes to dancing, but I can run like the wind."

"I'm no exercise junkie. I'm more of a homebody."

"Did I mention I'm hung like a horse?"

"Now, you're talking! Meet me at the stable."

John H. Dromey was born in northeast Missouri, USA. He enjoys reading—mysteries in particular—and writing in a variety of genres. In addition to contributing to the Black Hare Press series of Dark Drabbles anthologies, he's had short fiction published in Alfred Hitchcock's Mystery Magazine, Martian Magazine, Mystery Weekly, Stupefying Stories Showcase, Thriller Magazine, Unfit Magazine, and elsewhere, as well as in numerous anthologies, including Chilling Horror Short Stories (Flame Tree Publishing, 2015).

Stitching Up the Mourning
by Terry Miller

Raymond stitched up the back of his new jacket. He worked hard the last few days so that it was perfect. Jessica always made sure everything fit, so he felt it was appropriate that he should honour her memory. Who dies of a heart attack at twenty-four?

Jessica's funeral was exhausting, mostly mentally. Everyone left the gravesite but for Raymond. What is appropriate in saying goodbye to one's beloved wife?

Raymond left the house with the jacket. Human flesh was surprisingly warm. It was only fitting that he remembered her with what they both loved best; him inside of her.

Terry Miller lives in Portsmouth, Ohio. His work has been featured in Sanitarium Magazine, Devolution Z, Jitter, Rhysling Anthology 2017, Poetry Quarterly, Sirens Call Ezine, The Horror Tree's Trembling With Fear, SpillWords, Organic Ink Vol. I, Curses & Cauldrons Anthology from Blood Song Books, Forest of Fear from Blood Song Books, the Dark Drabble Anthology Series from Black Hare Press, 100 Word Zombie Bites from Reanimated Writers Press, Scary Snippets, Guilty Pleasures & Other Dark Delights, 100 Word Horrors 3, and O Unholy Night In Deathlehem from Grinning Skull Press.
Facebook: tmiller2015
Amazon: amazon.com/author/millerterryl

If Only
by Nerisha Kemraj

I hear your name whispered in the winds.

I feel your touch as the sun kisses my skin.

Your warm embrace weaves its way into my soul, engulfing my thoughts with memories of yesteryear.

How my petals wish to brush against your eager lips.

And my fingers long to intertwine with yours.

My body yearns for you, an aching desire—unfulfilled.

Because you're no longer here.

Tears caress my cheeks as my heart fails to forget, your blood upon my hands.

A lament of sadness fills my ears as Death's song sings your name.

If only I hadn't killed you…

Nerisha Kemraj *resides in Durban, South Africa with her husband and two mischievous daughters. Writing since 2017, she has had over 100 short stories and poems published in various publications, both print and online. She has also received an Honourable Mention Award for her tanka in the Fujisan Taisho 2019 Tanka Contest. She holds a Bachelor's degree in Communication Science, and a Post Graduate Certificate in Education from University of South Africa.*
Amazon: amazon.com/author/nerisha_kemraj
Facebook: Nerishakemrajwriter

Faith's Passion
by Ximena Escobar

Faith closed her eyes to better feel his beautiful form; his ribs under her fingertips; his masculine torso narrowing until hips protruded like horns in her grasp. *I am yours*, she pledged in her silence, envisioning his eyes like heaven well up in a shared emotion. *Only you love me as much as I love you.*

Kneeling before him, her docile hands slid like petals down his legs. She opened her mouth and glided her kiss to his toes, nailed to a guilt bestowed upon her like an evil's curse. "Forgive me," she pleaded, "That I cannot heal your wounds."

Ximena Escobar is writing stories and poetry. Originally from Chile, she is the author of a translation into Spanish of the Broadway Musical "The Wizard of Oz", and of an original adaptation of the same, "Navidad en Oz", both produced in her home country. Since 2018 she has published several short stories in various anthologies and online platforms, and is now slowly working on her own collection. Ximena has a degree in Arts & Communication Science and lives in Nottingham with her family.
Facebook: Ximenautora
Twitter: @laximenin

Ghost
by Nicola Currie

Like that, you are gone. Number disconnected. Clothes taken. Photos of us torn, scattered on the floor like the confetti I dream of.

But like spirits, there are traces of you to be found. Your Facebook page is a spirit board; the only way we connect from the disparate realms of my love and your abandonment, though the energy only flows one way. I know my messages get through, until I cannot find you there either: all online presence vanished behind a veil, like thoughts of the dead lost to time.

Where do you wander, spirit? I will find you.

Nicola Currie is from Cambridge, UK where she works in educational publishing. She has published poetry in literary magazines, including Mslexia and Sarasvati, and short stories in various anthologies. She has also completed her first novel, which was longlisted for the Bath Children's Novel Award. Website: writeitandweep.home.blog

Carving into Your Heart
by Wendy Roberts

Screams fill the small cabin as Mia carves a basic arrow through the heart with their initials into Sam's shoulder. It's the only thing she's got time to create before blood loss is an issue, but Sam won't stop squirming.

"If you would stop moving, I'd be done already."

"Please," Sam pleads, trying to turn away.

"Please stop, I'm sorry."

"For what?" Mia grabs her chin so she'll face her. "You fell in love with someone else and that's fine. I'll just leave this little reminder of us. Won't that be nice?"

Sam slowly nods

"Good, now just hold still."

*Writing short stories and novels started as a past time for **Wendy Roberts** and has now become a fully fledged passion. She posts short stories on her website and can be found most days on Twitter.*
Website: flippinscribbler.com
Twitter: @_WARoberts

Stuffed
by Clint Foster

He took my love into a shipping container, away from anyone that might hear her screams or the sounds of his tools. There, he cut her open, slicing her with thin, sharp knives, and taking out her innards with painstaking precision, preserving them in jars. Then he filled her up with wool and wire, posing her like she was dancing, and put all of her makeup on just like she did. By the time I got her back, I could hardly even tell she was no longer alive, but at least now I will know she can never leave me.

Clint Foster *lives with his herd of four cats, beloved Basset, Zero, and wonderful wife, Nik. He loves to tell stories just as much as he loves to read them, and is excited to share his work. A longtime consumer of media of all kinds, he enjoys giving back what he hopes everyone else thinks are good stories. Facebook: ClintFosterAuthor*

The Succubus Queen
by Zoey Xolton

The prince stares, eyes wide, mouth open, breeches taught. He swallows, then licks his lips. Confined within the inverted pentacle of salt on his chamber floor stands a demon.

With eyes as black as night, she wears nothing but her long mane of dark hair. Her form is perfect in every way conceivable, though her milk-white flesh is inscribed with ancient runes and symbols of the occult.

"I am Lilith, Queen of the Legions of Hell," she declares. "What depraved pleasures does your dark heart desire, prince?" The alluring succubus smiles, revealing her sharp fangs.

"*All of them*," Zekiel whispers.

Zoey Xolton is an Australian Speculative Fiction writer, primarily of Dark Fantasy, Paranormal Romance and Horror. She is also a proud mother of two and is married to her soul mate. Outside of her family, writing is her greatest passion. She is especially fond of short fiction and is working on releasing her own themed collections in future.
Website: www.zoeyxolton.com

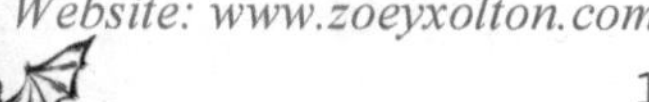

I Heart You
by Shawn M. Klimek

Blood striped Mandy's forearm like a barber pole and trickled from her bent elbow. In her fist, at eye-level, she clutched a purplish, human heart, still hot. Red droplets spattered her face as she shook it at Paul.

"This! This is what I will do to you if you ever cheat!"

Paul's gaze flitted anxiously between Mandy, the heart, the bloody knife in her left hand, and her ex-boyfriend, Daniel, lying on the floor.

"Suppose someone falsely accuses me of cheating," Paul challenged, unhappily.

"I would know!" Mandy insisted.

No. No, you wouldn't, Paul thought to himself. *I'm sorry, Daniel.*

Shawn M. Klimek is the middle child of seven creative siblings, a globetrotting, U.S. military spouse, an internationally best-selling short-story writer, award-winning poet, and butler to a Maltese. More than one hundred and fifty of his stories and poems have been published in digital magazines or anthologies, including BHP's Deep Space, Eerie Christmas and every book so far in the Dark Drabbles series.
Website: jotinthedark.blogspot.com
Facebook: shawnmklimekauthor

Deep Breaths
by Eddie D. Moore

John followed Cindy through the cornfield. A sheepish grin filled Cindy's face when they reached the centre of the field. John stepped into the small clearing and smiled as Cindy sat on a blanket. She patted the ground beside her.

"Lay down beside me. This is the most secluded and peaceful place I know of. No one will bother us here."

John did as Cindy instructed and took her hand gently in his. "The smell of dirt really turns me on."

Cindy took a deep breath and said, "Me too. It reminds me of all the bodies we've buried together."

Eddie D. Moore *travels hundreds of hours a year, and he fills that time by listening to audiobooks. When he isn't playing with his grandchildren, he writes his own stories. You can find a list of his publications on his blog or by visiting his Amazon Author Page. While you're there, be sure to pick up a copy of his mini-anthology Misfits & Oddities.*
Website: eddiedmoore.wordpress.com
Amazon: amazon.com/author/eddiedmoore

The Black Mass
by Zoey Xolton

"What're you doing in my chambers?"

The robed intruders rushed Kassia as she scrambled backwards in her canopied bed.

"Guards! Help me—" the princess screamed. Scarred hands closed around her throat, crushing her airways; then there was nothing but darkness.

When she awoke, she found herself shackled to a stone altar, surrounded by candles.

"Hear us, Dark Lord!" the lovers cried. "Accept this offering as a token of our devotion! Pure blood, as pure as our love for you! The way is open!"

Kassia's eyes flew upward, just in time to catch the cruel glint of a ceremonial blade.

Zoey Xolton *is an Australian Speculative Fiction writer, primarily of Dark Fantasy, Paranormal Romance and Horror. She is also a proud mother of two and is married to her soul mate. Outside of her family, writing is her greatest passion. She is especially fond of short fiction and is working on releasing her own themed collections in future.*
Website: www.zoeyxolton.com

Faller?
by A.L. Paradiso

"Worth sneaking past the rangers onto the Grand Canyon's glass walkway? Let's climb over the glass wall. I hope your life insurance is paid up." She grinned.

"Stop kidding about that! Let's not, and say we did it."

"I'm climbing over. CHICKEN!"

"Shelly, don't… Damn it. OK. I'll hold you. No! Don't lean over. That sudden stop at the bottom's gruesome. If you fall, I get double indemnity. Come back."

"Come on, join me, Al. CHICKEN!"

"Ok. Ok. H-h-here I come. Hold me. Don't let me fall."

"Don't be silly. Spread your arms like this."

"Why the grin? S-s-s-h-h-e-l-l-l-l-l-l-l-y-y-y…"

"Oops!"

A.L. Paradiso was born in Europe, English is his second language, following Italian—then Latin, Pig Latin, French and assorted computer languages. He lives in upstate NY with three cats. In college he took a dislike to writing of any kind and swore never to try that again. Some years later, influenced by Babylon 5's creator and his own pressure to write about two traumatic events, he turned to creative writing. As of Feb 2020, he has shared 130+ published stories with others online (> 4.6 million views), in eleven anthologies, DRAGON TALES COLLECTION, and two literary journals.

Amazon: www.tinyurl.com/Paradiso-dragons
Books2Read: books2read.com/ap/RWjj5e/AL-Paradiso

Love Restored
by Mikko Rauhala

The data vault cracks open beneath my fingertips. Thousands upon thousands of directories, millions upon millions of files. Only one you. A search on the user ID I found in your trash yields a few dozen hits, though. You've been diligent about updating your backups, darling.

The latest version of you has already met me. It didn't go over well. The next to last will suffice, with no memories to awkwardly paint over. It's still you; still beautiful, still vibrant, still mine.

I initiate the download and start preparing our virtual world, where digital oxytocin will make our bond mutual.

Mikko Rauhala is a Finnish author of speculative fiction with a national Atorox award nomination under his belt. Informed by his master's degree in intelligent systems, Rauhala is most at home in hard science fiction settings, though he's not exclusive and likes to cross genres. Rauhala has dabbled in editing flash fiction for The Self-Inflicted Relative anthology, and some of his English science fiction can be found in the Infinite Metropolis short story and audio drama collection, co-authored with Edmund Schluessel.
Blog: rauhala.org
Podcast: infinitemetropolis.com

Sitting Ducks for Cupid
by John H. Dromey

At the urging of her friends, a lonely woman gave online dating a try. Eventually, she identified a likely prospect.

After a reasonable amount of electronic foreplay, she decided to take their relationship to the next level. She arranged for a face-to-face meeting. Along with other body parts, however, she got cold feet and sent her clone on the first date with instructions to charm her suitor, if possible, and assess his intentions.

The suspicious male first-time dater dispatched a clone of his own to check out whoever showed up for the tryst.

Their clones found true love and eloped.

John H. Dromey was born in northeast Missouri, USA. He enjoys reading—mysteries in particular—and writing in a variety of genres. In addition to contributing to the Black Hare Press series of Dark Drabbles anthologies, he's had short fiction published in Alfred Hitchcock's Mystery Magazine, Martian Magazine, Mystery Weekly, Stupefying Stories Showcase, Thriller Magazine, Unfit Magazine, and elsewhere, as well as in numerous anthologies, including Chilling Horror Short Stories (Flame Tree Publishing, 2015).

Taking the Plunge
by Nicole Little

My new husband planned our honeymoon to the last detail. Our calendar was blocked; we had little free time. It was a bit annoying, but love was in the air. We drank too much, danced too much; Eli finally started to relax.

On our last night I suggested a stroll in the fresh ocean air. It wasn't on his itinerary, but after some convincing, we set off hand-in-hand.

I'm not exactly sure why I pushed him off the cliff.

The look on his face as he plunged over the side told me it was one thing he *hadn't* planned on.

Nicole Little *is an award winning short story writer living in St. John's, Newfoundland, Canada. Her publishing credits include Sweet Sixteen (Kit Sora: The Artobiography, 2019), The Market and Last One Standing (Dystopia from the Rock, 2019); Far Out and On a Wing and a Prayer (Flights from the Rock, 2019). Her short story Doxxed placed favorably in the Writers Alliance of Newfoundland and Labrador's "A Nightmare on Water Street: Scary Story Reading". In her spare time, Nicole can be found with either a pen in her hand or her nose in a book. She is married with two daughters.*

Blood-Mate
by Vonnie Winslow Crist

Canines showing, Lilith whispered, "It's best to love someone before making him your blood-mate." Then, staring into his eyes, she leaned forward and bit Percy's neck.

He gasped. After a second of pain, warmth surged through his veins. It was like whiskey going down the throat or heat as one sat by the fire. Then it was fire. Percy felt more alive—as if he'd been living a half-life until that moment.

"Now, you're eternally mine," said the vampire.

Though he'd barely noticed her before, Percy was now mesmerised by Lilith.

He thought, *If this isn't love—it's close enough for me.*

Vonnie Winslow Crist is author of The Enchanted Dagger, Owl Light, The Greener Forest, Murder on Marawa Prime, and other award-winning books. Her fiction is included in "Amazing Stories," "Cast of Wonders," "Outposts of Beyond," Killing It Softly 2, Defending the Future - Dogs of War, Midnight Masquerade, Chaos of Hard Clay, and elsewhere. A cloverhand who has found so many four-leafed clovers she keeps them in jars, Vonnie strives to celebrate the power of myth in her writing.
Website: www.vonniewinslowcrist.com

Girl's Best Friend
by Nicole Little

If you asked Rachel, cats were a girl's best friend. Strays just seemed to seek her out. It was hard to walk past those furry little faces: sad, cold and lonely. So, she brought them home and loved them.

As their numbers climbed, her apartment grew smaller and smaller. A cat was always underfoot. Rachel was bled dry buying litter and cat food. Her paycheques quickly dwindled…and so did the kibble. So, when one day, Mittens tripped Rachel at the top of the stairs, well, the cats weren't too sad about it.

They had plenty to eat now.

Nicole Little is an award winning short story writer living in St. John's, Newfoundland, Canada. Her publishing credits include Sweet Sixteen (Kit Sora: The Artobiography, 2019), The Market and Last One Standing (Dystopia from the Rock, 2019); Far Out and On a Wing and a Prayer (Flights from the Rock, 2019). Her short story Doxxed placed favorably in the Writers Alliance of Newfoundland and Labrador's "A Nightmare on Water Street: Scary Story Reading". In her spare time, Nicole can be found with either a pen in her hand or her nose in a book. She is married with two daughters.

Like I Do
by C.L. Williams

I know you have been unfaithful to me. I've seen you talking to other guys, giving them the smile you once gave me.

That is OVER!

None of them will ever love you the way I love you. I will take each of them out, gone for good. I know all of them will break your heart, and I am the one who completes you.

I will end them, I will bury them, and you will soon forget those other men and we will have the ultimate fairytale ending.

Until then, I have bullets to buy and holes to dig.

C.L. Williams is an international best-selling author currently living in central Virginia. He has written eight poetry books, four novellas, one novel, and a contributor to a multitude of anthologies and magazines. His most recent anthology appearance ANGELS: Dark Drabbles #2 from Black Hare Press became a number one in hot new releases. C.L. Williams is currently working on his second novel and a new poetry book. Facebook: writer434 Twitter: @writer_434

Tonight
by Brandi Hicks

She pulled Trevor's profile up on her phone and swiped through the pictures, smiling to herself. She squirmed in her driver's seat, rubbing herself, while looking at his photos, coming to a climax as she saw the front door of the house across the street open. Trevor and his wife stepped out. She hated his wife. He was too good for her, and tonight he'd see that, he'd see his mistake. She looked in the backseat to check that she had everything—duct tape, rope, Rohypnol, knife. Yes, tonight he would see his mistake. Tonight, he will finally choose her.

*Growing up in West Virginia, **Brandi Hicks** loved to have her nose in a book, her eyes toward the night sky and putting a pen to paper. Her imagination was always sparked by her grandfather and her mom taking her to new places and teaching her about the unusual. She loves fantasy, sci-fi, and learning about science and history. She has two beautiful children, and hopes to instil creativity and a love of reading in them. Finding new crafts to try keeps her busy when not playing with her kids or working.*

Night Sweats
by Ann Christine Tabaka

Here I am, Barbara called in her sleep. *Here I am*, he answered. Was this a dream, or was he really there, lying right beside her? She awoke covered in sweat, gasping for breath. It all felt so real.

She remembered how it used to be with his warm body next to hers. Aroused, she got up and retreated to the shower. Lathering up, she imagined his touch, his soft lips against hers, and his hands caressing her breasts. She did not need him.

As the warm water poured over her, heightening her senses, it called out, "Here I am."

Ann Christine Tabaka was nominated for the 2017 Pushcart Prize in Poetry, has been internationally published, and won poetry awards from numerous publications. She is the author of 9 poetry books. Christine lives in Delaware, USA. She loves gardening and cooking. Chris lives with her husband and two cats. Her most recent credits are: Burningword Literary Journal; Ethos Literary Journal, North of Oxford, Pomona Valley Review, Page & Spine, West Texas Literary Review, The Hungry Chimera, Sheila-Na-Gig, Pangolin Review, Foliate Oak Review, Better Than Starbucks!, The Write Launch, The Stray Branch, The McKinley Review, Fourth & Sycamore.

One More Drop
by Jo Seysener

Your lips, red like Snow White's, that perfect pout. I want to keep you like this forever. Pristine. You want this date to be our last; I am sure by the way your eyes flick away when I speak.

Rage simmers as I tip the vial in my hand over your glass. Is it horror that I'm making an advance? Red blooms, creeping up your neck, covering your discomfort as you sip.

Soon you will be perfect forever, frozen in this moment. Your eyes already dull, I witness your confusion, struggling to lift the glass.

Go on, just one more.

***Jo Seysener** is a mum of three crazies, a scatter of chickens, a decrepit kelpie and a rambunctious GSD. She lives with her husband near Brisbane, Australia. When she is not exposing her kids to cult story books from her childhood, she can be found in the kitchen experimenting with new flavours and pairings. She adores alpacas.*
Facebook: joseysener
Website: www.joseysener.com

12

by Chris Bannor

They said he could never understand love because love was from the heart. How could a machine with a metal body and circuit-board view of the world comprehend the greatest mystery of the human experience?

How could he not try though? The heart, with all its mythos, was the most enigmatic puzzle. A muscle like any other, and yet to humanity it was the home of the soul, the provider of love.

He looked around the room, blood and bodies strewn around like so much jetsam. You needed a heart to love? That was okay then. He now had 12.

Chris Bannor is a science fiction and fantasy writer who lives in Southern California. Chris learned her love of genre stories from her mother at an early age and has never veered far from that path. She also enjoys musical theater and road trips with her family but is a general homebody otherwise.
Facebook: chrisbannorauthor
Website: ChrisBannor.com

He'd Do It Again
by Gabriella Balcom

"What's it like outside?" Miles asked.

"Black like my true love's heart," his wife Sonia kidded, winking at him.

He grinned, but wondered if she suspected. If she found out, he hoped she'd love him, anyway. After all he'd done it for her.

Reaching for his hand, she placed it over her heart, tenderly kissing him. "It beats for you alone. And because of you."

That lay Miles' doubts to rest. He'd killed a man to get her that organ, but had no regrets. Sonia would've died without it. Given the chance, he'd do the same thing again.

Gabriella Balcom lives in Texas with her family, loves reading and writing, and thinks she was born with a book in her hands. She works in a mental health field, and writes fantasy, horror/thriller, romance, children's stories, and sci-fi. She likes travelling, music, good shows, photography, history, interesting tales, and animals. Gabriella says she's a sucker for a great story and loves forests, mountains, and back roads which might lead who knows where. She has a weakness for lasagne, garlic bread, tacos, cheese, and chocolate, but not necessarily in that order.
Facebook: GabriellaBalcom.lonestarauthor

Felicia
by Vonnie Winslow Crist

Dom missed Felicia. He missed how they used to hold hands, kiss first thing in the morning and last thing at night, and share a mug of coffee.

On Dia da los Muertos, Dom packed a strand of Felicia's hair, thermos of coffee, candle, and matches in a sack and headed for the graveyard.

Once there, he sat before Felicia's headstone, lit the candle. Then, holding her hair, he summoned his wife while the Veil was at its thinnest.

When a worm-infested Felicia pushed up from her grave ready for a kiss, Dom steeled himself—for her lips were gone.

Vonnie Winslow Crist is author of The Enchanted Dagger, Owl Light, The Greener Forest, Murder on Marawa Prime, and other award-winning books. Her fiction is included in "Amazing Stories," "Cast of Wonders," "Outposts of Beyond," Killing It Softly 2, Defending the Future - Dogs of War, Midnight Masquerade, Chaos of Hard Clay, and elsewhere. A cloverhand who has found so many four-leafed clovers she keeps them in jars, Vonnie strives to celebrate the power of myth in her writing.
Website: www.vonniewinslowcrist.com

The Crimson Vendetta
by Delaney McCormick

"You're late," Sergeant DeMarco growled, snatching the crimson umbrella from Alessandra's hand.

Turning onto Fifth Avenue, the pair made small talk as Alessandra bent suddenly to adjust her stocking. She counted silently while seven shots pierced the night and the man beside her stumbled and fell into the street, his blood seeping into the gutter with the rain. Standing, Alessandra crushed the sergeant's hat under her stiletto heel before she ducked into the shadows.

"Well done, my love," Salvatore whispered as he took Alessandra in his arms and kissed her passionately. "Three more to go. You'll need a new umbrella."

Delaney McCormick is a poet, storyteller, and observer of life. Born in a small Utah town, her mother taught her at an early age to love the beauty in art, photography and the written word. She graduated with honors from a local University with a focus in Psychology. When she is not writing, she can be found catering to the whims and wishes of her four rescue animals.

Never
by S.N. Graves

Never liked sushi. Fish makes me queasy. But she loves it, and I love her, so now I do.

Never thought much of family. But she loves them, and I love her, so I smile.

Never done well with "fathers." But she loved him once, and I love her, so I am polite.

Until I'm not...

Never killed a man before. Violence makes me cringe. But he hurt her, and I love her, so I squeeze.

Until my fingers ache, until the pops and cracks of Daddy's neck bones drown out the desperate, whistling gasps from his suffocating trout lips.

S.N. Graves was born in the South and can't see calling anyplace without a Waffle House home. She earned her M.F.A. in Popular Fiction from Seton Hill University in 2014 and was a senior editor at Loose Id LLC. She is twenty-three years happily married to the self-proclaimed victim of Stockholm syndrome, Brian David Graves, and enjoys duct taping her two adult sons to a chair and forcing them to read all the ugly first drafts of her books. Graves also freelance edits and creates art, including book covers.
Website: www.sngraves.com
Facebook: Shannon.N.Graves

I Wear an Invisibility Cloak
by Shelly Jarvis

Her curls are like a golden halo glowing around her head. When she walks by, the rest of the world turns to black and white, shades of grey, easy to ignore, when she is full of colour. I taste her with my eyes.

I want to run my fingers through those curls. I want to trace the lines of her neck to the hollow at her collarbone, feel the soft skin where it dips.

"Julie," she asks, "why do you have my pillow?"

I smile and shrug as I pass my roommate her pillow. At least she knows my name.

Shelly Jarvis is a speculative fiction author from West Virginia, US. She found a life-long love of sci-fi and fantasy in the 3rd grade when she found Madeleine L'Engle's "A Wrinkle in Time." Shelly is an avid reader, a Whovian, the ideal viewer of dog rescue videos, and undoubtedly Ravenclaw. She currently has three YA sci-fi books available for purchase on Amazon. Website: www.ShellyJarvis.com

Come Home
by James Lipson

Sometimes, when you're gone, I think you're never coming home. I don't know what to do when you're not here. The house is quiet, and your smell fades. I hear your voice and see your face, but you're not here and I don't know why. I hope you come home soon.

Normally when you leave, you give me bye-bye food and tell me you love me. This time the bright lights men carried you away while you were sleeping. I said goodbye, but I don't think you heard me. I hope you come home, I'm hungry and I miss you.

James Lipson's debut book, Fallen and Other Stories, was published in 2019. His short stories have appeared in Black Hare Press Anthologies, Teleport Magazine, Inner Circle's Writers Group Anthologies, and others. With a background in art, James has naturally turned to illustrating as he writes, bringing many of his short stories to life not only with descriptive detail, but also detailed visual imagery.
Website: www.jameslipson.com
Instagram: jameslipsonart

Alone Again
by Ann Christine Tabaka

Martha spends all of her afternoons alone and lonely. Many empty hours are now filled with the endless memories of a life that was once so vibrant. She used to know love. It seems like so many years ago when he left her for another.

Now all her dreams have turned to dust. She sweeps them under the rug, along with her shattered hopes and ambitions. Words are now her only friend.

So Martha loses herself in romance and adventure novels, living what is left of her life in her books. She becomes just another character in someone else's dream.

Ann Christine Tabaka was nominated for the 2017 Pushcart Prize in Poetry, has been internationally published, and won poetry awards from numerous publications. She is the author of 9 poetry books. Christine lives in Delaware, USA. She loves gardening and cooking. Chris lives with her husband and two cats. Her most recent credits are: Burningword Literary Journal; Ethos Literary Journal, North of Oxford, Pomona Valley Review, Page & Spine, West Texas Literary Review, The Hungry Chimera, Sheila-Na-Gig, Pangolin Review, Foliate Oak Review, Better Than Starbucks!, The Write Launch, The Stray Branch, The McKinley Review, Fourth & Sycamore.

The First Time
by K.T. Tate

You always remember the first time. It was perfect. The night air was warm, fireflies illuminated my way. Candles gently lit the grove, rose petals scattered. I'd chosen you. From all the options, you stood out the most. Wise, strong, generous. I was smitten.

Laying on the altar, painted with your symbols, I started the chant. I gasped as you manifested upon me, smoky, multi-limbed, burning. I fell right then and there. I saw my love reflected in your many obsidian starlit eyes. I wept with joy as you branded my soul, claiming me, and I knew this was forever.

K.T. Tate lives in Cambridgeshire in the UK. She writes mainly weird fiction, cosmic horror and strange monster stories. Website: www.eldritch-hollow.com

The Sound of Dirt and Freedom
by Neen Cohen

I heard the *thunk* as mother threw her handful of dirt on my grandmother's coffin. The rain hadn't yet started but I could smell it in the air.

Silence now filled the car.

I heard that *thunk* again in my head.

I looked to my mother, our hands entwined on the leather seat between us and my uncle's bald head in the driver's seat.

She smiled, and her eyes shone.

I smiled back and knew I would always love that *thunking* sound.

She would never know how far I went to make sure she never heard that woman's abuse again.

Neen Cohen lives in Brisbane with her partner, son and fur babies. She is a writer of LGBTQI, dark fantasy and horror short stories and has a Bachelor of Creative Industries from QUT. She can often be found writing while sitting against a tombstone or tree in any number of graveyards.
Website: wordbubblessite.wordpress.com/
Facebook: neen.cohen.82

The WOW Factor
by John H. Dromey

Kay returned from vacation to find the secretarial pool abuzz with gossip about the office Lothario's latest conquest.

"I'm shocked that Helen would have anything to do with a womaniser like Doug," someone said.

"How do you know she did?" Kay asked.

"He has proof. Doug's been showing off the text messages they exchanged. He asked Helen what she thought of the evening they spent together, and she responded with the single word: WOW!"

"The joke's on Doug then," Kay said.

"How so?"

"Helen loves old Elmer Fudd cartoons. In place of LOL she keys WOW: waffing out wowd."

First published in *Flashshot*, 2012

John H. Dromey was born in northeast Missouri, USA. He enjoys reading—mysteries in particular—and writing in a variety of genres. In addition to contributing to the Black Hare Press series of Dark Drabbles anthologies, he's had short fiction published in Alfred Hitchcock's Mystery Magazine, Martian Magazine, Mystery Weekly, Stupefying Stories Showcase, Thriller Magazine, Unfit Magazine, and elsewhere, as well as in numerous anthologies, including Chilling Horror Short Stories (Flame Tree Publishing, 2015).

Bubbling Over
by A.R. Johnston

"He loves me, he loves me not, he LOVES ME!" she squealed as she plucked the last petal from the flower. Dropping it into the pestle with a flourish. She giggled and danced around the room.

"He will love me!" she crowed, scaring the poor sleeping dog on the floor, and all she could do was laugh more.

She bounced back to the pestle and bubbling pots on the stove. She ground the petals and added them to the bubbling pot.

"He will definitely love me now, and he'll leave her for me. Everything will be as it should be."

A.R. Johnston is a small-town girl from Nova Scotia, Canada. She is known to write mostly urban fantasy, though she goes where the muses lead her and you never know where that may be. She is a lover of coffee, good tv shows, horror flicks, and a reader of good books. She pretends to be a writer when real life doesn't get in the way. Pesky full-time job and adulting!
Facebook: arjohnstonauthor
Website: arjohnstonauthor.wordpress.com

Love Him More
by Cassandra Angler

Killing with him was so much fun. The way his dark eyes glowed black as the twinkle of life in theirs fades. The way his brown hair shimmered with the crimson mixture of sweat and blood. He never let me play, though. That was a problem. He was distracted with the kill, my own hunt unnoticed. Only when he stood, panting and weary, did he notice the knife in my hand. Eyes wide and alarmed, he fell, shrieks escaping him as I plunged the knife into his chest. I loved him before, but as a corpse I love him more.

Cassandra Angler is a married mother of four who lives in the State of Ohio in the USA. When she isn't busy caring for her family, Cassandra works on her upcoming novel due out in November of 2020 titled Contaminated. Cassandra has three short story publications as well as several flash fiction and drabble publications.

Feelings in Low Ground
by Ximena Escobar

A fine leather string circled loosely the slender hand, hanging below the protruding wrist-bone. A plait, like a black snake, ran tight down the back, hollowed by the cold wetness of hair lingering within the knots. A chill spread down his back too as he pulled the plait, and his gold rings glistened.

Her black eyes knew to look at him the way he wanted. There was a balance somewhere between the sustain inside them and his urge to hurt her; love was that balance, stronger than restraint; stronger than guts knotting themselves in a slave-owner's stomach, like black snakes.

Ximena Escobar is writing stories and poetry. Originally from Chile, she is the author of a translation into Spanish of the Broadway Musical "The Wizard of Oz", and of an original adaptation of the same, "Navidad en Oz", both produced in her home country. Since 2018 she has published several short stories in various anthologies and online platforms, and is now slowly working on her own collection. Ximena has a degree in Arts & Communication Science and lives in Nottingham with her family.
Facebook: Ximenautora
Twitter: @laximenin

The Curse Reborn
by Matthew M. Montelione

It was Necho's fault that Helen was dead. He did it out of love. He pined for her for so long; it was his turn to be happy. Necho performed the ritual very carefully, whispering ancient words to put Helen's body into shock and wrestle her soul from the depths of time.

She would once again be reborn, this time through the curse: the old spell that he went under over two thousand years ago. Helen would understand, once she remembered that during his reign over Egypt, she was his beloved princess of the Nile. They could be happy again.

Matthew M. Montelione is a horror writer and American Revolution historian born and raised on Long Island in New York. His work has been published in many titles, including MONSTERS: A Horror Microfiction Anthology, Quoth the Raven: A Contemporary Reimagining of the Works of Edgar Allan Poe, Thuggish Itch: Devilish, WHAT IF?: History Rewritten, Long Island History Journal, and Journal of the American Revolution. Matthew lives with his wife in New York. Website: maybeevils.com
Facebook: maybeevils

No More
by Jennifer Hatfield

"For years I've waited for you," Jonnie growled into Shawn's ear as he pushed him to his knees and encircled his neck with his arm.

Gasping for air, Shawn choked out the words, "You. Know. I. Like. Girls."

"I won't wait anymore. I love you." With a quick snap of the neck, Jonnie whispered, "Goodbye."

He struggled to lift the dead weight into the trash chute, then snuck into the apartment. He grabbed a pair of boxer shorts and Shawn's class ring to save as mementos. He casually left the building. Finally free to find another target for his adoration.

Jennifer Hatfield spent a large portion of her life being a dedicated mother and wife. She managed her epilepsy diagnosis, and handled the loss of her husband. Grateful to find comfort in the ability to write in an effort to express her feelings, thoughts, and struggles. She's published 5 poems.

As Needs Must
by Kimberly Rei

"Please," she begged, "I need you."

Tears coursed down her cheeks, dripping off her chin and into the etched silver goblet. I carefully brushed damp curls of hair away. It simply wouldn't do to lose precious droplets. I nuzzled her forehead and tightened my grip on her neck. When she tried to gasp, I shivered.

I had met her only a few months ago, and she fell as the first snow in winter. Soft, graceful, and absolutely pure.

She stopped crying. The goblet glowed with a tender light, her life now in my hand.

"I need you, too, my sweet."

Kimberly Rei has been writing for as long as she can remember. At five years old, her parents gifted her with a set of Children's Classics that she had no hope of reading. Yet. The potential alone sparked a love of words that has never wavered. Kim has taught writing workshops and edited novels for Authors You May Recognize. She has published several short stories and now can't stop chasing paper dragons. She currently lives in Tampa Bay, Florida with her wife and an abundance of gorgeous beaches to explore.

Until Your Death Do Us Part
by Peter J. Foote

"Nurse, how long does she have?"

"Sir, that information is for family only."

"I'm her hus…husband's great-nephew. I wanted to say goodbye."

"I shouldn't, but you'd better hurry. She doesn't have long," the nurse says, but the man has already entered the room.

"Ruth? It's Issac, can you hear me?" The young looking man pulls a chair to the bed. "I'm sorry it took me so long to get here, you know how I lose track of the years."

Ancient eyes flutter open. "Husband?"

"Here, my love."

"My dashing husband, forever young. Hold my hand."

"Always my love."

Peter J. Foote *is a bestselling speculative fiction writer from Nova Scotia. Outside of writing, he runs a used bookstore specialising in fantasy & sci-fi, cosplays, and alternates between red wine and coffee as the mood demands. His short stories can be found in both print and in ebook form, with his story "Sea Monkeys" winning the inaugural "Engen Books/Kit Sora, Flash Fiction/Flash Photography" contest in March of 2018. As the founder of the group "Genre Writers of Atlantic Canada", Peter believes that the writing community is stronger when it works together.*

Twitter: @PeterJFoote1

Website: peterjfooteauthor.wordpress.com

The Feeling is Mutual
by Nikki DeKeuster

"Are these necessary?" I jangled the handcuffs.

Detective Weis glanced over. "No."

My stomach rumbled, and he unwrapped a heart-shaped box on the bed, stealing a truffle. "Your boyfriend isn't very original."

I winced. "He's not my boyfriend anymore."

"Does that absolve you?" He sneered. "Bureau can stop this psychopath *without* your help. He's gotta sleep; we don't."

"Insomnia makes you careless, Detective."

His muscles locked in living rigor mortis.

"You forgot I despise chocolates." Smiling, I caressed his cheek. "No worries. My fiancé is as excited to see you as you are to see him."

Nikki DeKeuster devours souls. She spits them onto her glowing screen and toys with their lives for your amusement. Reading this story makes you an accomplice to their suffering. You're welcome. A storyteller with decades of experience crafting tales with her friends, she's bound some of them to bring into the wider world. The stories, not her friends. She enjoys throwing stones into Lake Michigan with her daughter and keeping her husband up past his bedtime with her ramblings. The first novel in her horror series will claw its way out of the earth in 2020.
Website: NJDeKeuster.com

Dedicated
by Serena Jayne

You wrote the novel for "the one who got away" as though your lover's heart simply sprouted wings and flew from its cage. Vanity overcomes reason and I, for one blessed moment, allow myself to believe I'm the beloved treasure you mourn losing. A never-ending pain you need to numb. An absence that shreds your soul.

The fragile construct of my delusion collapses and sorrow crushes my joy, for I never escaped. My desiccated heart remains entombed within your stronghold, cobweb-covered and cursed; forlorn and forgotten. I will be forever dedicated to you, yet your dedication, as always, lies elsewhere.

Serena Jayne is a graduate of Seton Hill University's Writing Popular Fiction MFA Program. Her short fiction and poetry can be found in Switchblade Magazine, the Drabble, Crack the Spine Literary Magazine, 101 Fiction, the Oddville Press, and other publications.
Website: www.serenajayne.com
Twitter: @SJ_Writer

Obsession
by A.R. Dean

I'd never thought I would love a woman until I met you. Blond hair and curves. Your flawlessness shines brighter than the sun.

I dye my frizzy brown locks. I diet and exercise until our sizes match. I love her enough to become her.

I go crazy knowing that it's only the hall that separates her apartment from mine. I play when she's away. I roll around her bed and touch her things to gather the scent.

She's surprised to see me. I make it quick. Like a deer, I bleed her out. In her blood, we will become one.

A.R. Dean is a dark and twisted soul. Dean has spent their whole life spreading fear with the tales from their head. Best known for stories that terrify and show the evilest side of human nature. So, look for Dean haunting your local cemetery or under your bed, because they're here to spread the fear. Turn off your lights and enjoy a scare. Dean is being published in Black Hare Press's Beyond and Unravel Anthologies. Keep a lookout for more stories.
Facebook: A.R. Dean Author & Ghoul

Flowers
by Chris Bannor

They speak of love like it's beautiful. They write sonnets and ballads and plays about endless pining and hopeful romance. They don't understand the gnawing, devouring hunger though.

Love is an ache that breathes in my lungs, a burning that sinks into my skin until there is only one way to end my suffering.

I must suffocate it.

This must be hard for you to understand. You bought their lies. You believe in fairytales and flower-strewn dreams.

The best I can give you though, my love, is a bed to rest your head on and fresh flowers for your grave.

Chris Bannor is a science fiction and fantasy writer who lives in Southern California. Chris learned her love of genre stories from her mother at an early age and has never veered far from that path. She also enjoys musical theater and road trips with her family but is a general homebody otherwise.
Facebook: chrisbannorauthor
Website: ChrisBannor.com

Golden Hour Killing
by T.W. Garland

Against the brick wall, she is social media perfection. Her smile brazen. Her eyes coy. Taking the picture, he shakes with eager anticipation.

Her hand falls, by design. The dripping adds a leading line. She bites her lip.

It must be right. Hold it. Capture the moment. Bind it tight with duct tape.

Beyond the camera are style bloggers, how-to vloggers, followers and influencers. They need updates.

Blood runs from the knife in her hand, dripping on the victim. Spurts of blood slow from the neck wound.

She looks behind the camera, smiling at him. Together they make a killing.

T.W. Garland has a stack of Victorian novels that taunt him with their unbroken spines. He has published stories containing monster hunters, supernatural creatures, steampunk adventurers, aberrations of nature, crazed criminals and psychic detectives. He buys more books than he could hope to read and is glad not to have been born in the nineteenth century or in a novel by Dickens. One day he hopes to live in the real world.
Website: twgarland.wordpress.com

Long Haul Space Love
by Mason Harold Hilden

Joshua was dying.

After 342 years of space-transport, Joshua looked to be in his nineties due to countless hyper-sleeps. His co-pilot and lover for three centuries, Moira, woke him, his vitals deteriorating. His final act, to make love one last time.

Their coupling ended, Joshua rested his head upon Moira's breasts as she ever-so-lightly scratched his back. He died minutes later.

Moira rose from the bed, and Joshua's head unceremoniously fell onto the sheets. She contacted her employer, Bacchus Robotics, and notified them that her contract was now terminated, and a limited production Moira-7000 was once again on the market.

Mason H. Hilden is a Bluenoser, who currently resides in Saint John, New Brunswick, with his family. Over the last twenty years, he has written comic-books, including one professional work. He has also dabbled in mini-biographies, interviews, baseball articles, and animation scripting. Mason recently began writing fiction, and believes that BHP may have created a monster by accepting his submissions.

The Baum Squad
by John H. Dromey

"I'm a wizard of OZ," Mike told the woman next to him.

She took her drink and hurried away.

"Why not say you're a successful commodities trader?" his friend Joey chided him. "Not many people recognise OZ as the trading symbol for oats."

"I want to downplay my Wall Street connection."

"You're hopeless," Joey said. "I'm going to circulate."

A smiling woman took his place.

"Is it true? You're a wizard?" she asked Mike.

"Sort of," he said.

"What a coincidence. I have an uncle who's cowardly around lions. Sort of. He's allergic to cats."

"Buy you a drink?"

"Sure."

John H. Dromey was born in northeast Missouri, USA. He enjoys reading—mysteries in particular—and writing in a variety of genres. In addition to contributing to the Black Hare Press series of Dark Drabbles anthologies, he's had short fiction published in Alfred Hitchcock's Mystery Magazine, Martian Magazine, Mystery Weekly, Stupefying Stories Showcase, Thriller Magazine, Unfit Magazine, and elsewhere, as well as in numerous anthologies, including Chilling Horror Short Stories (Flame Tree Publishing, 2015).

Plans
by T.W. Garland

Every morning, she walks to her car like a bride down the aisle. I watch her get ready, eat her breakfast, collect her things, but it's that walk and the look in my direction that reminds me why I love her. She is my princess, and life without her is unimaginable.

Then there is that smug guy across the street. He's always looking at her. Some mornings I catch him twitching the curtains, watching her leaving.

I've got plans for him. Once he's gone, I won't be watching through binoculars and she'll be walking in my house, not his house.

T.W. Garland *has a stack of Victorian novels that taunt him with their unbroken spines. He has published stories containing monster hunters, supernatural creatures, steampunk adventurers, aberrations of nature, crazed criminals and psychic detectives. He buys more books than he could hope to read and is glad not to have been born in the nineteenth century or in a novel by Dickens. One day he hopes to live in the real world.*
Website: twgarland.wordpress.com

Afterthought
by Andrew Anderson

As the petals fall from the rose, they become a decaying vestige of her existence. It was the last thing they'd bought together, neither of them knowing its significance at the time.

Now, as Lori disposes of the detritus, she's also laying to rest those fragments of memory. Sometimes her nose cruelly tricks her into thinking that Alicia is still alive.

The room still holds her sillage, as if she's only just passed through it. Hopeful, Lori blindly chases its scent, forgetting once again that she cannot be with Alicia.

Lori should have thought of that, before she killed her.

Andrew Anderson is a spare-time writer of microfiction, flash fiction and short stories, from Bathgate, Scotland. His work has been published on FlashFlood and Re:Written, and published in Black Hare Press anthologies.
Twitter: soorploom

Free to Love
by J.A. Hammer

It was a problem. Neither of them were sleeping through the night, and he was much more tired than when he used to play videos games until the wee hours. She couldn't drink coffee and begrudged him his morning cuppa, glaring daggers over the table as she nibbled plain toast and he chewed scrambled eggs. Their love was frozen.

Thankfully, he knew how to return to normal. The christening pillow, pale blue with navy stitching, was a perfect size. He tossed it into the crib. Pressed down steadily. And...problem solved. Now they were free to love each other again.

J.A. Hammer is a coffeeholic in the wild concrete city of Tokyo. Known online as CoffeeQuills, they are a multi-genre writer who enjoys a wide range of speculative fiction. Previous publications include Apocalypse and Unravel by Black Hare Press and Trembling with Fear Year 2 by the Horror Tree. To catch up on future 2020 projects (a LitRPG serial and a superhero romance), feel free to find them on Twitter and at their website.
Website: www.coffeequills.com
Twitter: @coffeequills

Christmas Present
by Glenn R. Wilson

"Here, open yours first," I say as I hand it to her.

"What's in it?"

"Something you never expected."

At this, she can't wait. Her fingers tear at the wrapping paper. In a moment, she's flipping up the lid of the box. One look inside, and she's all over me with hugs and kisses.

"Now we can get married," I exclaim.

She takes her deceased mother's wedding ring gently into her hands. The ring her father had refused to give us. The ring that sat cradled in his severed hand placed within.

"Well, he did say over his dead body."

Glenn R. Wilson has come full circle. Making a point to mature, like fine wine, before diving head-first into his long list of writing projects, he's approaching them with a plan. That strategy is to build with one brick at a time. He's accumulated a few bricks already and is adding more. Over time, with persistence and determination, he'll have a home. But for now, a solid foundation is the goal. Please, enjoy the process with him.

In Love and War
by Steven Lord

"Never leave me again. Promise me."

He stroked her golden hair. "On the darkest nights, it was your face that brought me back. I'm not going anywhere."

She smiled, eyes glinting with unshed tears. "Sounds good to me."

She bounced out of bed and flung back the curtains. The sunlight streamed in, forcing him to first squint against the brightness, then close his eyes completely.

And he was back under the blood red sky, wrapped in dust and the screams of dying men. He looked down at his ruined body and cried, wishing he could slide into his dream forever.

Steven Lord is a debut author based in the south of England. He is currently attempting to cram writing in alongside a busy day job, with varying levels of success. While his long-term aspiration is to get a novel published, at present he would be pretty pleased with a drabble or two.

The Secret to Staying Young
by Jodi Jensen

"Hellooooo…?" Sybil's heart raced in anticipation. "Zane? I'm back."

When he didn't answer, she entered the bunker. He was right where she'd left him, hanging from his ceiling chains, body covered in gashes, only now his lips were contorted in frozen agony.

She quivered in delight at the full container beneath him.

Tonight, she'd bathe in blood and replenish her youth.

Sybil moved his body in with the others, smiling as her gaze flickered over the pile of unwitting donors. Each man had fallen under her spell, and she'd loved every one of them.

They'd kept her young, after all.

Jodi Jensen, *author of time travel romances and speculative fiction short stories, grew up moving from California, to Massachusetts, and a few other places in between, before finally settling in Utah at the ripe old age of nine. The nomadic life fed her sense of adventure as a child and the wanderlust continues to this day. With a passion for old cemeteries, historical buildings and sweeping sagas of days gone by, it was only natural she'd dream of time traveling to all the places that sparked her imagination.*
Twitter: @WritesJodi
Facebook: jodijensenwrites

And the Maiden
by Raven Corinn Carluk

Where could she be? Mors searched frantically through the village, heart racing with worry. None of the villagers knew where his Alba was, knew when they'd last seen her.

He found her at the base of a cliff, battered, broken, bleeding.

Mors knelt beside Alba, tears in his eyes, words stuck in his throat. He couldn't fix her, put her bones where they belonged, nor ease her pain.

"I threw myself down so you'd release me. You must do your job, take lives. The world needs Death."

He swallowed his sob, closed her eyes, and carried Alba's soul to Elysium.

Raven Corinn Carluk writes dark fantasy, paranormal romance, and anything else that catches her interest. She's authored five novels, where she explores themes of love and acceptance. Her shorter pieces, usually from her darker side, can be found in Black Hare Press anthologies, at Detritus Online, and through Alban Lake Publishers.
Twitter: @ravencorinn
Website: www.ravencorinncarluk.com

All for Love
by Eddie D. Moore

The grasshopper squirmed as Jacob pushed it against the largest thorn on the blackberry vine. When he let go, he kept his hand ready to catch the insect if it tried to get away.

Leah squatted down beside Jacob. "Good job, Jacob. You got one on every thorn."

Jacob looked deep into Leah's eyes. "What about my reward?"

Leah pressed her lips against Jacob's for several seconds. "See that barbed wire fence?"

Jacob nodded.

"There's more where that came from if you put a frog on every barb."

Jacob kissed Leah's cheek and promised, "It'll be ready in the morning."

Eddie D. Moore travels hundreds of hours a year, and he fills that time by listening to audiobooks. When he isn't playing with his grandchildren, he writes his own stories. You can find a list of his publications on his blog or by visiting his Amazon Author Page. While you're there, be sure to pick up a copy of his mini-anthology Misfits & Oddities.
Website: eddiedmoore.wordpress.com
Amazon: amazon.com/author/eddiedmoore

Fake Reality
by Kaitlyn Arnett

"Maya, why are so many people staring at us?" Alora asked the charming girl sitting next to her. The stares burned like hundreds of eyes following her, and her alone.

Maya smiled; the sad, bitter look foreign on her bright features. "Because they see the truth, my love."

"The truth?" Alora echoed. The words sounded as though they should come from a horror story, far away from this ordinary place.

"Yes, my angel. They see my truth."

"And what is that?"

Maya's smile grew strange, startlingly unfamiliar. "That I only exist inside your head, my darling."

And Alora's reality shattered.

Kaitlyn Arnett is a teen author who has been writing for five years. She focuses on the fantasy and thriller genres, specifically drabbles and short stories.

Hands Up
by Shelly Jarvis

She's in it for the money, I'm in it for the love. Neither of us will get what we want from this. But we keep it going, ignoring our differences and the inevitable heartache. That's a problem for future me. Present me is having a blast.

She's putting on her mask, tightening her holster. I can't help but watch her, forgetting my preparations. She's a force.

She goes in blasting, commanding, and the bag of money is in her hands before I even see the guard. He shoots and I block her, watching her escape as my love bleeds out.

Shelly Jarvis is a speculative fiction author from West Virginia, US. She found a life-long love of sci-fi and fantasy in the 3rd grade when she found Madeleine L'Engle's "A Wrinkle in Time." Shelly is an avid reader, a Whovian, the ideal viewer of dog rescue videos, and undoubtedly Ravenclaw. She currently has three YA sci-fi books available for purchase on Amazon. Website: www.ShellyJarvis.com

His Perfect Ending
by Monica Schultz

Kadin glances at the time on his phone, smiling as Chloe's face lights up his screen. Too easy to save her profile picture. And screenshot her Instagram stories. And sneak pictures during class.

21:15.

Right on time, Chloe clocks off from work. She waves goodbye without checking the rapidly darkening streets.

Kadin sticks to the shadows, following at her heels. Chloe clutches her keys in a white-knuckled fist.

Chloe pauses when the cars come into sight. Her blue bug. His white van.

She breaks into a sprint, but cheerleaders aren't fast.

And Kadin has already turned all the security cameras.

Monica Schultz is a full-time Mathematics and History teacher from Ipswich, Australia, with a passion for writing fantasy. When she isn't busy finding 'x' in the latest equation, you can find her curled up with a young adult book and a cat on her lap. Website: https://monicaschultzauthor.weebly.com/ Instagram: @monicaschultzauthor

Little Dove
by Drew Starling

Emma cradled her newborn in her arms. She sang to him. Swaddled him. Eskimo kissed his little nose. Their nightly ritual of love.

All she ever wanted to be was a mother. And she was. Finally. After so many years of trying.

"Happy birthday, my little dove. Can you believe it? Fourteen years." She kissed his forehead. "And no one can take that away."

She placed him back in the shoebox. Put the box back in the bag. Put the bag back in the freezer. Closed the freezer door and left the garage.

"Coming!" she called upstairs to her husband.

Drew Starling is an author of horror and dark fiction. His short stories have been published in over a dozen anthologies and his collaborative novel "Storming Area 51: Horror at the Gate" spent time ranked as Amazon's #1 Sci-Fi Anthology. His only rule of writing is the dog never dies.
Website: www.drewstarling.com
Twitter: @ScaryStarling

Sharing is Caring
by Andrew Anderson

We sat in the spaceship's canteen.

Jim, grinning, reached for my plate. I hit his fingers with my fork.

"Ow! Marie, come on—"

"Jim, if you wanted astro-fries, you should have printed yourself some."

Jim sulked.

Later, we hugged and made up, and I administered his sleeping medication—two doses.

The next day I watched from the crew lounge window as Jim drifted off into space, his face apoplectic behind his spacesuit's visor.

I made a hand heart, blew him a kiss and mouthed, "I love you."

I do still love Jim, but not enough to share my food.

Andrew Anderson is a spare-time writer of microfiction, flash fiction and short stories, from Bathgate, Scotland. His work has been published on FlashFlood and Re:Written, and published in Black Hare Press anthologies.
Twitter: soorploom

Sharpest is the Kiss That Pops
by Joachim Heijndermans

Yeah, I know what it looks like. A joke. A skit for chuckleheads. But it's true. I, the bitch made of blades, love her. And she, that plump balloon, loves me back.

How do we do it? It's almost like a dance. I blow her kisses, which lifts her into the air. She bounces past me and pirouettes on her toes. I mime my fingers grazing her rubber hide, never touching lest she pops.

Do I want to touch her? Fuck, yes I do. But it's all right. We laugh and love, we cry and shout. We make it work.

Joachim Heijndermans *writes, draws, and paints nearly every waking hour. Originally from the Netherlands, he's been all over the world, boring people by spouting random trivia. His work has been featured in a number of anthologies and publications, such as Mad Scientist Journal, Asymmetry Fiction, Hinnom Magazine, Ahoy Comics's Edgar Allan Poe's Snifter of Terror, Metaphorosis and The Gallery of Curiosities, and he's currently in the midst of completing his first children's book.*
Website: www.joachimheijndermans.com
Twitter: @jheijndermans

Captivated
by Terri A. Arnold

I've never felt more complete than I do right now. I gently brush aside the lock of hair that has fallen across her face. She looks so beautiful and innocent in sleep.

I can't help but place a firm kiss to her lips in hopes that she'll wake. She stirs slightly, and my hands go to her, turning her face towards me. It takes a moment before her eyes focus, first a look of confusion in her eyes, followed by fear.

"Shhh, sweetheart, it's just me," I murmur in her ear as she struggles against the restraints holding her down.

Terri A. Arnold is an avid reader turned writer from a small town in Nova Scotia, who has spent her life reading and wishing she was writing. Although she has written a lot in those years, she has only recently begun to submit pieces for publication. With ongoing encouragement from family and writing challenges with friends, Arnold felt the urge to try her hand at publishing.

Love Letters
by Dawn DeBraal

Robert took the knife, digging deep into the bark. Instead of initials, she insisted he spell out their names. Robert didn't want to get caught defacing a tree, but he was in love. The trunk was hard. His tongue stuck out as he dug in deep. He was proclaiming their love. He'd only carved, "Robert Loves C" when the knife slipped, slitting Cassandrialina's throat. Horrified, Robert ran off. Months later, he met Cici, the new woman of his dreams.

"For me?" Cici squealed when he took her to the park. He had finished the name when no one was around.

Dawn DeBraal lives in rural Wisconsin with her husband Red, two rat terriers, and a cat. She has discovered that her love of telling a good story can be written. Published stories with Palm-sized press, Spillwords, Mercurial Stories, Potato Soup Journal, Edify Fiction, Zimbell House Publishing, Clarendon House Publishing, Blood Song Books, Black Hare Press, Fantasia Divinity, Cafelit, Reanimated Writers, Guilty Pleasures, Unholy Trinity, The World of Myth, Dastaan World, Vamp Cat, Runcible Spoon, Dark Christmas, Siren's Call, Iron Horse Publishing, Falling Star Magazine 2019 Pushcart Nominee.
Amazon: amazon.com/Dawn-DeBraal/e/B07STL8DLX

Condo at Front Beach Road
by Stephanie Scissom

Gone.

My daughter was gone, taken from our vacation in Florida. From the ocean, I'd seen her walk toward the road.

"She forgot her phone," her sister informed me.

Maybe I waited too long to check on her. In the condo's parking lot, I found one flip-flop, but Allie was gone.

Was it the man by the pool? A construction worker who'd leered at my 17-year-old? Would I ever know?

Year after year, I returned to stand in that ocean and stare at the last spot I'd seen her.

As waves crashed around me, I wished I was gone, too.

***Stephanie Scissom** hails from Altamont, TN. She works nights in a tire factory and plots murder by day. She's currently working on a twisted apocalyptic trilogy starring Lucifer and his tortured wife.*
Facebook: stephaniescissom2019

Sacrifice
by N.M. Brown

My daughter Hallie's life was stolen from her at only eight years old. She was run over by a drunk driver while walking home from school.

A lady came by the house after they took her body, said she had the ability to make it right. But at a cost. I sobbed as I told her how little money I had. The woman smiled, told me she had no use for money.

I signed my name in blood across the paper. The woman cackled and disappeared.

Hallie's laughter's heard from her bedroom, but I've no soul left to enjoy it.

*Since **N.M. Brown** made her first post to a popular Internet forum, she's taken the horror community by storm. Her ability to create, terrify, and drive home her stories is insurmountable. N.M. Brown's published works can be found in multiple anthologies for all to read, but be forewarned, if you do... you may want to call your therapist after, her stories are terrifying, disturbing and devilishly unsettling. She is not only a fright visually, but also has a creepy tentacle in horror podcasting as well. Sinister Sweetheart writes, voice acts and is the media director of the Scarecrow Tales podcast.*
Website: Sinistersweetheart.wixsite.com/sinistersweetheart
Facebook: NMBrownStories

Star-Crossed
by Raven Corinn Carluk

They met at midnight on the border of their two clan territories, two shadows amidst the darkness.

Hiro sighed in relief. "I worried you wouldn't make it."

Toshi settled his pack, the younger shinobi glancing over his shoulder. "Mako was suspicious. I made sure he didn't follow." One hand strayed to his katana.

Far too late to turn back, Hiro gave no voice to doubts. He would do anything for Toshi, including run from both their clans for the rest of their days.

He tucked a strand of hair behind Toshi's ear. All worth it to wake in his arms.

Raven Corinn Carluk *writes dark fantasy, paranormal romance, and anything else that catches her interest. She's authored five novels, where she explores themes of love and acceptance. Her shorter pieces, usually from her darker side, can be found in Black Hare Press anthologies, at Detritus Online, and through Alban Lake Publishers.*
Twitter: @ravencorinn
Website: www.ravencorinncarluk.com

Love Hearts
by Tracy Davidson

For our anniversary, my wife wants love hearts scattered across the bed. A dozen. Redder than roses. Fresher.

What my wife wants, she gets.

They couldn't be fresher. The last still throbs in my bloodied hand, its former host convulsed in death throes.

I leave the corpses. The dogs will eat well today.

I bear my basket of love up to our bedroom. My wife waits, the bed ringed by candles and her favourite toys.

I scatter my gifts before she chains me. Our white satin sheets and bare skin turn scarlet, slick with blood and sweat. And true love.

Tracy Davidson lives in Warwickshire, England, and writes poetry and flash fiction. Her work has appeared in various publications and anthologies, including: *Poet's Market, Mslexia, Atlas Poetica, Writing Magazine, Modern Haiku, The Binnacle, A Hundred Gourds, Shooter, Journey to Crone, The Great Gatsby Anthology, WAR* and *In Protest: 150 Poems for Human Rights.*

All Mine
by N.M. Brown

There he is again, lingering over us like a dry cough.

She's too polite to be unkind. But if she doesn't ask him to leave, I'll be forced to do it myself. She knows she is all mine.

They're in the kitchen now, having sent me away for the night. He says he needs to steal my girl to talk finances over dinner.

He has an allergy to shellfish, and I've rubbed shrimp all over his dinner plate and wineglass. There will be no magic pen or telephone to save him.

I utter a final greeting upon leaving.

"Goodnight, Dad."

*Since **N.M. Brown** made her first post to a popular Internet forum, she's taken the horror community by storm. Her ability to create, terrify, and drive home her stories is insurmountable. N.M. Brown's published works can be found in multiple anthologies for all to read, but be forewarned, if you do... you may want to call your therapist after, her stories are terrifying, disturbing and devilishly unsettling. She is not only a fright visually, but also has a creepy tentacle in horror podcasting as well. Sinister Sweetheart writes, voice acts and is the media director of the Scarecrow Tales podcast.*
Website: Sinistersweetheart.wixsite.com/sinistersweetheart
Facebook: NMBrownStories

The Badlands
by Chris Butler

She's one hell of a waitress. I watch her. She takes the orders while I knock back a few. She makes me remember I should stay off the booze.

Love from a distance is easy. It only hurts when you get close. So why am I sitting here, just to be near her?

Damn, her apron strings I would love to undo.

I walked through the badlands to get here. In this place, I saw something that could, I don't know, be a way back?

Her eyes are brown, and lovely. But I wonder, does she know mine are blue?

Chris Butler lives in the UK. His published fiction includes the novel Any Time Now, the novella The Flight of the Ravens (which was shortlisted for the BSFA award) and short fiction published in Asimov's Science Fiction, Interzone magazine, and The Best British Fantasy 2014.
Website: cbutlerwrites.wordpress.com

How to Win the Battle
by Michael D. Davis

Love, a fickle, horrible thing that no one can live without. I've struggled with it, like anybody. Won a battle or two here and there to earn the bruises on my time-worn heart. It was today, however, that I finally became victorious overall. I will no longer have to wander out into the blood strewn fields where the struggle between love and loneliness is fought. No, I have become triumphant in the ways of the heart; no longer will I be alone at night, just me and my thoughts. I now have the dear corpse of my darling for company.

Michael D. Davis was born and raised in a small town in the heart of Iowa. Having written over thirty short stories, ranging in genre from comedy to horror from flash fiction to novella he continues in his accursed pursuit of a career in the written word.

Hello Dear
by Jason Holden

The prisoner transfer truck screeched to a halt. A young mother, covered in blood, staggered towards it. Her infant in one arm, the other under her bloody coat.

"Help me. Please!"

The guard opened the door and was met by a silenced pistol. It flashed twice, once for each guard.

Wiping off the fake blood, she made her way to the back. Opening the door while staying hidden she tossed the doll. It was realistic enough to distract the guard, only for a second. That was all she needed.

From his seat in the back, her husband smiled.

"Hello, dear."

Jason Holden is a human. He lives here and there in the UK, always with his wife, daughter and fur baby. His primary goal is to raise his daughter to adulthood without any major damage. When he can, he writes. He thinks he does it well, but you can be the judge of that. He has been published in a few anthologies here and there, has been praised and put down for his writing. You can find and follow him on Facebook, although he asks you only follow him on Facebook and not through the streets. That's just creepy.
Facebook: Jason Holden-Author

The Last Supper
by Dale Parnell

Till death do us part.

I always struggled with that line. Marriage is forever, I truly believe that. Of all people, you knew me best, Eric. Did you really think I was going to let a little thing like death keep us apart?

Fifty-seven years together, that's a long time to prepare, to learn the skills. I have everything I need; good, sharp knives and saws, a strong, sturdy blender and a beautiful brand-new crock pot. I've got so many recipes that I want to try, there won't be an ounce of you wasted.

And we can be together forever.

Dale Parnell lives in Staffordshire, England, with his wife and their imaginary dog, Moriarty. He has self-published two collections of short stories, "The Green Cathedral" and "Bramble and other stories". Dale also writes poetry, and is lucky enough to have pieces featured in several poetry and fiction anthologies.
Facebook: shortfictionauthor

The Golden Years
by Trisha Ridinger McKee

Sylvia pressed her hand against the cage, jumping back when he lunged. There were few similarities between Alex, her husband and Alex, the brain-dead monster that would not think twice before chewing on her face.

Their retirement was to be full of trips and adventures. Not terror. Sylvia had not known anything was amiss the day Alex left to get his fishing license.

But now she was faced with a choice. Grow old without her love. Or hope that his kind had a bond among them. As she unlocked the cage and swung upon the door, she braced herself.

Trisha Ridinger McKee *resides in a small town in Pennsylvania where love has proven to be a problem. Her work has appeared or is forthcoming in publications such as Tablet Magazine, The Oddville Press, Crab Fat Literary Magazine, Night to Dawn Magazine, Deep Fried Horror, 4 Star Stories, and more.*

Endless Love
by David Bowmore

We met online before our first date. He was a gentleman and respected me totally.

On the second date, I was a little more relaxed. We went a little further.

I went back to his place after our third date. While we were relaxing in the afterglow, he said, for the first time, that he loved me. I was shocked; well it was a bit soon for those sorts of words. We broke into fits of laughter.

That was five years ago.

Every day, John Smith comes down here into the dark cellar and tells me that he loves me.

David Bowmore has lived here, there and everywhere, but now lives in Yorkshire with his wonderful wife and a small white poodle. He has worn many hats in his time; head chef, teacher and landscape gardener. His first collection of short stories 'The Magic of Deben Market' is available from Clarendon House.
Website: davidbowmore.co.uk
Facebook: davidbowmoreauthor

Juvenile Love
by Kelly A. Harmon

"If you love me, help me kill my grandfather," Chelsea said.

Lips firm, the swipe of Paul's tongue through Chelsea's mouth sealed the deal. "I love you—we'll kill my parent's after."

Chelsea nodded. "And then you'll kill me."

Paul hugged her tight. "My birthday gift to you."

His switchblade was old, but sharp. He handed her a hammer. Chelsea crept into the bedroom, swung the hammer hard. Blood spurted. Paul's knife slipped on the geezer's neck, slick with blood.

Grandpa lived.

The headline:

GIRL, 14, CHARGED AS ADULT WITH ATTEMPTED MURDER; BOYFRIEND, 13, CHARGED AS JUVENILE.

Ah, young love.

Kelly A. Harmon *is an award-winning journalist and author. She is a member of the Science Fiction & Fantasy Writers of America and the Horror Writers Association. A Baltimore native, she writes the Charm City Darkness series. The fourth book in the series, In the Eye of the Beholder, is now available. Find her short fiction in many magazines and anthologies, including Occult Detective Quarterly; Terra! Tara! Terror! and Eerie Christmas.*
Website: kellyaharmon.com
Facebook: Kelly-A-Harmon1

Tattoos
by G. Allen Wilbanks

"We're going to get matching tattoos!"

"What?" asked Bella, surprised by the announcement.

"As a sign of our love," continued Steve. "We'll tattoo each other's names on our arms. It's romantic."

Steve rolled up his sleeve and held out his arm for Bella to see. The name "Andrea" was inked onto his left forearm and then crossed out with a black "X."

"Me and my last girlfriend did it. See?"

"I don't want your name tattooed on my arm," Bella told him.

"That's okay," said Steve, slipping a rag and a bottle of ether from his pocket. "Neither did Andrea."

G. Allen Wilbanks is a member of the Horror Writers Association (HWA) and has published over 100 short stories in various magazines and on-line venues. He is the author of two short story collections, and the novel, When Darkness Comes. Website: www.gallenwilbanks.com Blog: DeepDarkThoughts.com

Burn the World
by Zoey Xolton

"Do you love me?" Skullface asked.

"Yes."

"Would you do anything for me?"

"I would."

"Then prove your love to me. Push the button and destroy the world for me. Kill every last man, woman and child. Every beast that walks and flies upon the Earth. Kill them all, for me."

Aboard the privately funded space station, Marionette grinned from ear to ear as they stood before the control panel; Earth visible as a distant blue orb.

"For you, my king, anything," and then, pulling her man in for a kiss, she sat her pert derriere on the detonation panel.

Zoey Xolton is an Australian Speculative Fiction writer, primarily of Dark Fantasy, Paranormal Romance and Horror. She is also a proud mother of two and is married to her soul mate. Outside of her family, writing is her greatest passion. She is especially fond of short fiction and is working on releasing her own themed collections in future.
Website: www.zoeyxolton.com

Banshee
by Lyndsey Ellis-Holloway

She was alone. Now that he was gone, her life was over.

Tears flowed from her eyes as she wept, her throat raw as she screamed in anguish, her chest aching.

Her fingers clawed the freshly dug earth, her mournful cry leaving her breathless, her lungs burning, straining.

Her left arm went numb, her right hand clutching her chest as her heart shattered. The world went black, a thought crossed her mind that she would see him soon, on the other side.

But her wails only intensified.

Slowly she stood, jaw distended, dead eyes wide. Her mournful howl deafening.

Forevermore.

Lyndsey Ellis-Holloway *is a writer from Knaresborough, UK. She writes fantasy, sci-fi, horror and dystopian stories, focussing on compelling characters and layering in myth and legend at every opportunity. Her mind is somewhat dark and twisted, and she lives in perpetual hope of owning her own Dragon someday, but for now she writes about them to fill the void... and to stop her from murdering people who annoy her. When she's not writing she spends time with her husband, her dogs and her friends enjoying activities such as walking, movies, conventions and of course writing for fun as well! Website: theprose.com/LyndseyEH*

Till Death Do Us Part
by G. Allen Wilbanks

"Till death do us part. What a silly concept. Don't you agree, dear?" Ellie prattled on as she placed Victor's lunch on the table. Victor did not respond. He sat quietly with his newspaper propped up in front of him.

"I mean, who came up with that nonsense in the first place? As if death is some sort of ending, or an excuse to leave."

Victor slumped forward, his head coming to rest on his plate. The newspaper fluttered to the floor. Ellie calmly pulled him upright and returned his paper to his lap.

"Nope. You're not going anywhere, darling."

G. Allen Wilbanks is a member of the Horror Writers Association (HWA) and has published over 100 short stories in various magazines and on-line venues. He is the author of two short story collections, and the novel, When Darkness Comes. Website: www.gallenwilbanks.com
Blog: DeepDarkThoughts.com

My Team
by A.R. Dean

I love football. My team is the Williamstown Wolves. They're the greatest NFL team. My house is decorated in the team colours. Win or lose, I'm true to my team.

I brimmed with excitement when I got tickets to the game against our rivals, the Pelicans. We lose in overtime, and my heart is broken.

I reach the parking lot where some Pelican fans are celebrating their lucky win. "Wolves suck!" someone screams as he throws an empty beer can at my head.

Furious, I turn and open fire. I don't let one escape. You don't disrespect a man's team.

A.R. Dean is a dark and twisted soul. Dean has spent their whole life spreading fear with the tales from their head. Best known for stories that terrify and show the evilest side of human nature. So, look for Dean haunting your local cemetery or under your bed, because they're here to spread the fear. Turn off your lights and enjoy a scare. Dean is being published in Black Hare Press's Beyond and Unravel Anthologies. Keep a lookout for more stories.
Facebook: A.R. Dean Author & Ghoul

A Candlelit Shower
by Eddie D. Moore

The rain tapped lightly on the porch awning as the breeze spun the sail on the wind chime. Sarah took a sip of her wine and smiled at her husband. "I love the rain."

Kevin wedged the cork into the top of the bottle of Moscato. "I think you have told me that a few times over the years. Oh, if you listen close, you can also just hear the cries of our captives in the basement."

Sarah smiled. "You're just trying to get lucky by turning me on."

Kevin said softly into his wineglass, "You know me pretty well."

Eddie D. Moore travels hundreds of hours a year, and he fills that time by listening to audiobooks. When he isn't playing with his grandchildren, he writes his own stories. You can find a list of his publications on his blog or by visiting his Amazon Author Page. While you're there, be sure to pick up a copy of his mini-anthology Misfits & Oddities.
Website: eddiedmoore.wordpress.com
Amazon: amazon.com/author/eddiedmoore

The Greatest of Them All
by Chris Bannor

People wanted love. They would do anything for the idea of meeting that fated person and falling hopelessly, madly in love. There was no science for it, but people believed there should be. It made it easy to create some pseudo-science.

It became something no one expected. The online platform exploded and the classes to find a match were full moments after they were released. They used every method; expensive marketing campaigns, celebrity endorsements, even subliminal messaging. Fill out a form, take the classes, and you too can find your soul-mate.

Love was the most profitable scam of them all.

Chris Bannor is a science fiction and fantasy writer who lives in Southern California. Chris learned her love of genre stories from her mother at an early age and has never veered far from that path. She also enjoys musical theater and road trips with her family but is a general homebody otherwise.
Facebook: chrisbannorauthor
Website: ChrisBannor.com

Never Leave Me
by Peter J. Foote

The lantern casts wavering shadows in the cemetery until the light rests, illuminating the newly carved tombstone of Ian Sommers: "Untimely death, be at peace."

Wilhelmina sets the lantern atop her husband's tombstone and starts digging.

Smeared in mud and sweat, she only pauses when the shovel strikes wood. Shouting out in joy, Wilhelmina collapses to her knees.

Sweeping dirt aside until the brass plaque glitters in the soft moonlight and the words "Beloved husband" are visible.

Dirty hands caress the coffin lid. "You sought to escape me, but you'll be mine always." Rising, Wilhelmina pries open her husband's coffin.

Peter J. Foote is a bestselling speculative fiction writer from Nova Scotia. Outside of writing, he runs a used bookstore specialising in fantasy & sci-fi, cosplays, and alternates between red wine and coffee as the mood demands. His short stories can be found in both print and in ebook form, with his story "Sea Monkeys" winning the inaugural "Engen Books/Kit Sora, Flash Fiction/Flash Photography" contest in March of 2018. As the founder of the group "Genre Writers of Atlantic Canada", Peter believes that the writing community is stronger when it works together.
Twitter: @PeterJFoote1
Website: peterjfooteauthor.wordpress.com

The Reconciliation Gift
by Jasmine Arch

The old woman scuttled after us, pointing at the berries I'd picked.

"Gift." Finally, a word I understood amid the rapid-fire German babbling.

"Of course." I nodded and smiled. "It's for my mother-in-law. I need something to get the old bat off my back."

"*Das ist vergift*." She tried to grab them from my hands, but I pulled away just in time.

"Uh, Dad." My son plucked at my sleeve. "I think she means poison. Gift means poison in German."

"Course it does, kiddo." I grinned at him. "This German vacation your mum wanted is about to save my marriage."

Jasmine Arch lives in a rural corner of Belgium with two horses, four dogs, and a husband who knows better than to distract her when she's writing. Her love of the written word in all its forms and incarnations is only superseded by her deep abiding passion for caffein. Her work has appeared in Illumen Magazine, The Other Stories, Disturbed Digest, and Dark Moments.
Website: jasminearch.com
Twitter: @Jaye_Arch

Bittersweet
by Nerisha Kemraj

I got what I wanted
You left me alone
I didn't expect it
It cut to the bone

I begged you to leave
and yet you would stay
But one final push
and you went away

I wish you were here
Why did you listen?
You shouldn't have left
It was my indecision

The tables have turned
And now I'm free
But without you here
I cease to be

My nights have grown darker

My days are now cloudy

Because you took the sun

when you finally heard me

Bittersweet memories to treasure forever

Now that we're no longer together

Nerisha Kemraj resides in Durban, South Africa with her husband and two mischievous daughters. Writing since 2017, she has had over 100 short stories and poems published in various publications, both print and online. She has also received an Honourable Mention Award for her tanka in the Fujisan Taisho 2019 Tanka Contest. She holds a Bachelor's degree in Communication Science, and a Post Graduate Certificate in Education from University of South Africa.
Amazon: amazon.com/author/nerisha_kemraj
Facebook: Nerishakemrajwriter

Separated Again
by Patrick Winters

I'm missing my wife already. She was beautiful. Perfect.

Those diamond eyes that could kiss you with a stare and those luscious lips that could give you the real thing; her tickling fingers and her tiny toes; that adorable nose; her cute little ears, which she'd wiggle to make me laugh; those warm arms that would hold me in the day and those long, lovely legs that she'd wrap around my waist at night.

There wasn't a single part of her that I didn't cherish.

I admire each for one last time before I toss them into a garbage bag.

Patrick Winters is a graduate of Illinois College in Jacksonville, IL, where he earned a Bachelor of Arts degree in English Literature and Creative Writing and achieved membership into Sigma Tau Delta, an international English honors society. Winters is now a proud member of the Horror Writers Association, and his work has been published in the likes of Sanitarium Magazine, Deadman's Tome, Trysts of Fate, and other such titles. A full list of his previous publications may be found at his author's site.
Website: wintersauthor.azurewebsites.net/Publications/List

Lover's Leap
by G. Allen Wilbanks

William and Tracy held hands, gazing down at the rocky cliffside below them. Tracy inched closer to the edge to get a better look and whistled softly. It was a long way down.

When Tracy's dad had forbidden them from seeing each other, she had suggested running away and eloping. William was afraid her father would come looking for them and suggested a more permanent escape.

"We go on three," said William. "One…two…three!"

Tracy stood alone on the cliff, listening to William's screams as he fell. "I can't believe he actually did that," she muttered. "Dad was right."

G. Allen Wilbanks is a member of the Horror Writers Association (HWA) and has published over 100 short stories in various magazines and on-line venues. He is the author of two short story collections, and the novel, When Darkness Comes. Website: www.gallenwilbanks.com Blog: DeepDarkThoughts.com

Lindsay's True Love
by Stuart Conover

Blood splattered Lindsay's face.

Her heart pounding.

Another enemy fell before her blade.

The thrill of battle, the lust for blood.

It excited her unlike her lovers had.

Only Erika had moved her so.

It was no surprise she became one of Zenlan's finest knights.

With a never-ending war ahead of them, Lindsay would follow him until the end.

Even when the general across the battlefield was Erika.

Hours of fighting brought the two together.

The fighting as exhilarating as their love.

They drew in close.

Lips locked for one fleeting moment.

Before Lindsay thrust her blade into Erika's heart.

Stuart Conover *is a father, husband, rescue dog owner, published author, blogger, journalist, horror enthusiast, comic book geek, science fiction junkie, and IT professional. With all of that to cram in daily, we have no idea if or when he sleeps or how he gets writing done! (We suspect it has to do with having evil clones.) Stuart is a Chicago native and runs the author resource Horror Tree.*

Never
by Jasmine Jarvis

"I love you," I whispered to the little doll. "But I have to punish you for breaking my heart."

I look at the little calico doll in my hands. Its arms and legs hung limp, its black glass bead eyes stared straight up.

I took the needle and black thread and began to stich an X over its crooked red mouth. "You will never kiss another." I snipped the black thread, but I wasn't finished. I plucked its eyes off, "You will never look at another." I then plunged a hatpin into its heart, "and you will never love another."

Jasmine Jarvis is a teller of tales and scribbler of scribbles. She lives in Brisbane, Australia with her husband Michael, their two children, Tilly and Mish; Ripley, their German Shepherd, and indoor fat cat, Dwight K. Shrute.

A Mother's Love
by Jason Holden

Sarah came in from school practically skipping.

"Good day, dear?"

She threw her bag down and went to join her mum in the kitchen where she was chopping vegetables.

"It was great. You'll never guess. That kid that was bullying me has gone. His whole family just vanished, they're saying."

Sarah grabbed some carrot and crunched it on the way out of the room.

"Well, if it means you're happy again, then I'm glad."

She continued chopping and smiled, gazing out of the window she replaced the knife in its block; all the spaces were filled now, all except one.

Jason Holden is a human. He lives here and there in the UK, always with his wife, daughter and fur baby. His primary goal is to raise his daughter to adulthood without any major damage. When he can, he writes. He thinks he does it well, but you can be the judge of that. He has been published in a few anthologies here and there, has been praised and put down for his writing. You can find and follow him on Facebook, although he asks you only follow him on Facebook and not through the streets. That's just creepy.
Facebook: Jason Holden-Author

All for You
by K.T. Tate

I love you. I try to tell you, to express my desires. However, each time I do you look at me horrified, disgusted. Yes, our love is forbidden, but how can I resist you? I had to see you, touch you, let you know how I felt. I've watched you for so long.

I shouldn't have dragged your daughter into this, but I thought you'd listen if it came from her. This isn't working though. So, we'll wait for the priest to come and exorcise me from her body.

But don't worry, beautiful. I'll find a host you can love.

K.T. Tate *lives in Cambridgeshire in the UK. She writes mainly weird fiction, cosmic horror and strange monster stories. Website: www.eldritch-hollow.com*

Love Letters
by Nicola Currie

I liked what you wore yesterday, I type into instant messenger from my fake account. *Whore red suits you.*

A read tick appears, but she doesn't reply.

Where you off to today? I'll find you. Here's a picture I took yesterday. Slut.

I stop for now. My girlfriend's waiting to leave for our day at the beach.

What's wrong?" I ask as I join her in the hallway. "That creep bothering you again?"

I pull her close as her tears well.

"Don't worry, baby. I'd never let anyone hurt you."

She looks up at me, her eyes beaming with love.

Nicola Currie is from Cambridge, UK where she works in educational publishing. She has published poetry in literary magazines, including Mslexia and Sarasvati, and short stories in various anthologies. She has also completed her first novel, which was longlisted for the Bath Children's Novel Award. Website: writeitandweep.home.blog

Digging Up the Past
by Clint Foster

There are so many sensations to feel when I am around her, and I can never get enough of them. When I brought her back home, I wondered how she would fare. But we've done great. I've cleaned up all the dirt, and when I light enough candles, I barely notice the chemical smell. She doesn't eat like she used to and is somewhat less lively I admit. My makeup skills are getting better, but it's the way she sits, so stiff and postured, that reminds me most of when she was still warm. Nevertheless, I love having her around.

Clint Foster lives with his herd of four cats, beloved Basset, Zero, and wonderful wife, Nik. He loves to tell stories just as much as he loves to read them, and is excited to share his work. A longtime consumer of media of all kinds, he enjoys giving back what he hopes everyone else thinks are good stories.
Facebook: ClintFosterAuthor

Mrs. Malicious
by Gabriella Balcom

Biting her lip, fifteen-year-old Elabelle laboured over her exam.

"Take your time," her boyfriend Duane murmured. He always encouraged her. "You got this."

"No talking," their teacher, Mrs. Gray, snapped. Calling him up front, she paddled him hard. "Can't whine to daddy anymore," she commented, sneering.

Elabelle sent a gentle breeze to caress Duane's cheek when he sat down. She knew he hurt. In fact, he was heartbroken over his father's recent death. Focusing on their malicious teacher, Elabelle used a blast of air to knock her onto her bottom. "For you," she whispered to Duane.

He smiled.

Gabriella Balcom lives in Texas with her family, loves reading and writing, and thinks she was born with a book in her hands. She works in a mental health field, and writes fantasy, horror/thriller, romance, children's stories, and sci-fi. She likes travelling, music, good shows, photography, history, interesting tales, and animals. Gabriella says she's a sucker for a great story and loves forests, mountains, and back roads which might lead who knows where. She has a weakness for lasagne, garlic bread, tacos, cheese, and chocolate, but not necessarily in that order.
Facebook: GabriellaBalcom.lonestarauthor

Comeuppance
by Stephen Christie

"These fingers?"

Kelly nodded. Mickey picked up the tinsnips. Kelly's uncle Barry wailed through his gag, writhing around in the chair he was tied to. Barry's fingers came off with little effort from Mickey.

Barry's screams accompanied his blood hitting the floor.

Mickey pointed to Barry's crotch and looked at Kelly.

"No. He never did that to me," she said.

"Well... Lucky you, Barry," said Mickey.

"But he used to spy on me in the bath..."

Mickey tutted. He pulled out a penknife and forced open Barry's eyelids.

"I love you, Mickey."

"I love you too, baby."

Barry just screamed.

*A lifelong bookworm, cinephile, and wine connoisseur, **Stephen Christie** has decided to lay off the drink, and try his hand at a little creative writing of his own. A fan of Horror, Science Fiction, Military Fiction, and Historical Fiction, he hopes his years of enjoying a collection of great books will aid him in this new endeavour.*

Poisonous Love
by Nerisha Kemraj

Leia looked into his eyes as he lay sprawled across the bed.

"Drink this, you'll feel much better."

Danny clutched his abdomen, the intense pain not allowing him into an upright position.

"It's ok, I got you," Leia said, lifting his head onto her lap. "I love taking care of you."

Concern passed through Danny's eyes. He shouldn't have agreed to meet for a "final break-up dinner."

Leia applied a damp cloth to his forehead, hoping the potion would eradicate the poison from his system soon. Maybe she used a bit too much?

He had to stay alive.

For her.

Nerisha Kemraj resides in Durban, South Africa with her husband and two mischievous daughters. Writing since 2017, she has had over 100 short stories and poems published in various publications, both print and online. She has also received an Honourable Mention Award for her tanka in the Fujisan Taisho 2019 Tanka Contest. She holds a Bachelor's degree in Communication Science, and a Post Graduate Certificate in Education from University of South Africa.
Amazon: amazon.com/author/nerisha_kemraj
Facebook: Nerishakemrajwriter

Come Dance on My Grave
by J.B. Wocoski

My Necromancer danced naked on my grave, gyrating to entice me to rise again. I slept underground hearing our love song, "Come dance with me on your grave."

Clawing through my coffin lid, wanting to dance with her, naked, on the freshly turned earth above my grave. I pawed and burrowed through the dirt above, desiring her undead kisses, "Patience, my love. I am coming to you, keep dancing naked in the moonlight, I can only be with you before sunrise."

"Damn dawn!" I slip back down into my grave, praying she returns, enticing me to be alive once again.

J.B. Wocoski is the author and narrator of the shortstorypodcast.com with three flash fiction short story books published in the last three years. He is currently working on book 4 "Short Story Podcast 2019." He writes mostly science fiction, fantasy, and horror stories. He won the 2016 Little Tokyo Short Story Writing Contest with his short story "The Last Master of Go"
Website: shortstorypodcast.com

Keepsake
by Ximena Escobar

The time came to empty the dryer.

Crying on his t-shirt, breathing in the imperceptible particles of his scent, she lay on their bed–in the aching idea of his closeness, the unbearable reality of his loss. She paired his socks, folded his clothes. One last time.

She didn't draw his hand out of the washing bag. Just tied the excess fabric back with a hair-tie, making a fitted glove. Lying back on her pillow, she propped it between her legs, searching in the darkness for the man she once knew; with clean hands.

She didn't know who she'd killed.

Ximena Escobar *is writing stories and poetry. Originally from Chile, she is the author of a translation into Spanish of the Broadway Musical "The Wizard of Oz", and of an original adaptation of the same, "Navidad en Oz", both produced in her home country. Since 2018 she has published several short stories in various anthologies and online platforms, and is now slowly working on her own collection. Ximena has a degree in Arts & Communication Science and lives in Nottingham with her family.*
Facebook: Ximenautora
Twitter: @laximenin

A Killer Relationship
by V.L. Draven

We met at a bar. I knew she was special; it was in her eyes. We walked along the beach—talked. She revealed that she was an impaler, but I was a slicer. We didn't think it would work; we were so incompatible.

We killed alone, but we missed each other. I gave her blood-soaked roses. I learned the art of impalement, she the subtleties of the cut. Our victims screamed, but we drew closer.

We fell in love, but our families never approved; they said it wouldn't last. We married, and forty years later, we are still killing together.

V.L. Draven lives in Christchurch, New Zealand. He is a horror and dark fantasy writer, and is a regular contributor to fridayflashfiction.com. He has a number of larger projects currently in process, including several novels and short stories. When not writing he likes to escape into the windswept wilderness of the country of his birth, visit haunted houses, and dream of faraway places to visit.
Facebook: v.l.draven

Luna
by N.M. Brown

Some people say to do indulgence but in moderation.

But they haven't met Luna.

She's perfection incarnate. We're together all the time. We work together, sleep together, even take our trips to the bathroom together.

When we're apart, it's not good for us. There was a week where I feared I got too close. I distanced myself for a while. It was heartfelt agony.

She rushes to her window in anticipation, sensing me. As the curtains draw closed, I must remind myself that I'll do anything to protect our relationship.

Which is why she can never know who I am.

*Since **N.M. Brown** made her first post to a popular Internet forum, she's taken the horror community by storm. Her ability to create, terrify, and drive home her stories is insurmountable. N.M. Brown's published works can be found in multiple anthologies for all to read, but be forewarned, if you do... you may want to call your therapist after, her stories are terrifying, disturbing and devilishly unsettling. She is not only a fright visually, but also has a creepy tentacle in horror podcasting as well. Sinister Sweetheart writes, voice acts and is the media director of the Scarecrow Tales podcast.*
Website: Sinistersweetheart.wixsite.com/sinistersweetheart
Facebook: NMBrownStories

Sea Breeze Special
by Jodi Jensen

Jackson stared at the vial, mesmerised by the swirling pink liquid.

Every weekend, from behind the bar, he'd watched Veronica come in with friends and leave with a guy who wasn't him.

His visit to the witchdoctor was about to change all of that.

He dumped the love potion into the Sea Breeze cocktail she'd ordered, then served it to the woman of his dreams.

Tossing the drink back, she met his gaze over the rim of the glass.

Jackson took her home that night. "I've always loved you," he declared, tying her to his bed. "And now you're mine."

Jodi Jensen, author of time travel romances and speculative fiction short stories, grew up moving from California, to Massachusetts, and a few other places in between, before finally settling in Utah at the ripe old age of nine. The nomadic life fed her sense of adventure as a child and the wanderlust continues to this day. With a passion for old cemeteries, historical buildings and sweeping sagas of days gone by, it was only natural she'd dream of time traveling to all the places that sparked her imagination.
Twitter: @WritesJodi
Facebook: jodijensenwrites

Away From it All
by J.W. Garrett

The argument was the final straw.

"We're done!"

"Never." John towered over his wife, spilling his fifth drink of the evening. When she turned to leave, he tackled her, his glass slamming into her head, knocking her out cold.

She woke, groggy, her head bandaged and leg immobilised. "What did you do?"

"You fell. Fixed you up best I could."

"I can't move. I need a doctor." Her eyes widened, following his movements.

Spoon feeding her, he whispered, "Just us now. I'll take care of you. Always."

Gazing out the window, the whiteness blinded her. "Where…"

"Off the grid… Antarctica."

J.W. Garrett *has been writing in one form or another since she was a teenager. She currently lives in Florida with her family but loves the mountains of Virginia where she was born. Her writings include YA fantasy as well as short stories. Since completing Remeon's Quest-Earth Year 1930, the prequel in her YA fantasy series, Realms of Chaos, she has been hard at work on the next in the series, scheduled to release August 2020. When she's not hanging out with her characters, her favourite activities are reading, running and spending time with family.*
Website: www.jwgarrett.com
BHC Press: www.bhcpress.com/Author_JW_Garrett.html

Stuffed Love
by Michael D. Davis

I've only loved three people in my life. To some, that may sound not like very much, to others, that may be a hell of a lot. It depends on how lucky you've been. The first person on my list is my mother, one of the greatest people in the world. The second is a woman I've known since high school, Darla. She's one that accepts me just the way I am, faults and all. The third and final spot on my list goes to my son, Tod. They're my lovely family, perfectly preserved, stuffed and standing around the house.

Michael D. Davis was born and raised in a small town in the heart of Iowa. Having written over thirty short stories, ranging in genre from comedy to horror from flash fiction to novella he continues in his accursed pursuit of a career in the written word.

Soulmate
by Ximena Escobar

A shadow plunging in the periphery precedes a horrifying thud. The girl—spread and broken on the concrete—is still breathing. Blood gurgles out of her mouth as Eva lifts the back of her head, her own pain looking back at her through crystalline blue-grey eyes. The serpent tattoo on her clavicle is the same as that on the back of her own arm.

Desolation sweeps Eva's soul. In every landscape, every earthly creature, she'll seek the indelible imprint of the girl's fleeting gaze.

She'll only find it when she too hits the asphalt and looks to the light beyond.

Ximena Escobar is writing stories and poetry. Originally from Chile, she is the author of a translation into Spanish of the Broadway Musical "The Wizard of Oz", and of an original adaptation of the same, "Navidad en Oz", both produced in her home country. Since 2018 she has published several short stories in various anthologies and online platforms, and is now slowly working on her own collection. Ximena has a degree in Arts & Communication Science and lives in Nottingham with her family.
Facebook: Ximenautora
Twitter: @laximenin

Perfect
by Rachel Oram

It was love at first sight. He saw her across the crowded bar—such a cliché—but she was perfect. Long blonde hair, stunning smile, brilliant blue eyes. He approached and offered to buy her a drink. He was thrilled when she accepted.

Things went well to begin with; they chatted and laughed.

Later, she complained he was suffocating her. He tried to be gentle, but make-up would hide the bruises, make her perfect again.

He smiled as the embalming fluid slipped into her veins—she would join his collection of perfect women, none of whom would ever leave him.

Rachel Oram is a dabbling wannabe author and very occasional poet from the West Midlands. Her pets include a husband and two cats. She has attended several creative writing courses and has had a short story published in a charity anthology. One of her poems was published in Diverse Verse 2, a charity poetry anthology. Rachel loves reading and her taste tends towards horror and dystopian fiction. Her writing is also a little on the dark side to provide some light relief from her day job...

Rebound
by Michele Freeman

The scent of the gardenia candles wafted through the darkened room. Those tiny flames gave us the only light we needed.

"I love you," I whispered. "More than she ever did."

I saw the uncertainty in his gaze. I put my finger to his lips. "I know. You said your heart was too damaged to return my feelings."

I leaned over the bed and tenderly tightened the ropes on his wrists. "Don't worry, darling. I found you a new heart." I opened the cooler and showed him the organ I'd liberated from a less worthy man. "You'll love me soon."

*Award-winning author ***Michele Freeman*** writes horror and dark fiction. She loves crochet, chocolate, and zombies. She lives in Texas with her Viking husband and their adorable fur babies.*
Website: www.authormichelefreeman.com

A Good Mother
by N.M. Brown

My son requires a…special diet. There's a hunger inside of him; a darkness that, if left unsatiated, would swallow him whole.

As much as it breaks me, I've no choice but to help him. I love him. I'm a good mother, that's what we do.

Animals helped at first, but it was too heart-breaking. I gained employment at a mortuary, bringing home odds and ends. That worked for a while.

But he's getting older now, and his tastes are changing. He's decided only fresh is the best. I only pray the meat slicer's loud enough to cover up the screaming.

*Since **N.M. Brown** made her first post to a popular Internet forum, she's taken the horror community by storm. Her ability to create, terrify, and drive home her stories is insurmountable. N.M. Brown's published works can be found in multiple anthologies for all to read, but be forewarned, if you do… you may want to call your therapist after, her stories are terrifying, disturbing and devilishly unsettling. She is not only a fright visually, but also has a creepy tentacle in horror podcasting as well. Sinister Sweetheart writes, voice acts and is the media director of the Scarecrow Tales podcast.*
Website: Sinistersweetheart.wixsite.com/sinistersweetheart
Facebook: NMBrownStories

Consequences
by Galina Trefil

"I'd die for you. I'd kill for you," she promised him. But that wasn't what he needed…at least, not at first. But then he became terribly, painfully ill. With each passing day, she realised more and more that her beloved would be better off lying peacefully in the grave than suffering daily in life.

She explained this logic to him, after she fed them both a poison-laced final meal. "We will leave this world now," she beamed up at him, "together."

He blinked in horror at her announcement, suddenly all too-aware that his playing sick to get attention had consequences.

Galina Trefil is a novelist specializing in women's, minority, and disabled rights. Her favorite genres are horror, thriller, and historical fiction. Her short stories and articles have appeared in Neurology Now, UnBound Emagazine, The Guardian, Tikkun, Romea.CZ, Jewcy, Jewrotica, Telegram Magazine, Ink Drift Magazine, The Dissident Voice, Open Road Review, and the anthologies "Flock: The Journey," "First Love," "Sea of Secrets," "Coffins and Dragons," "Organic Ink volume One," "Winds of Despair," "Waters of Destruction," "Curses & Cauldrons," "Unravel," "Hate," "Love," "Oceans," "Forgotten Ones," "Dark Valentine Holiday Horror Collection," and "Suspense Unimagined."
Website: galinatrefil.wordpress.com
Facebook: Rabbi-Galina-Trefil-535886443115467

Sleep
by Christina Wilder

My husband was serene as he rocked back and forth on the stretcher, smiling as the ambulance careened down the city streets. The concoction I gave him already had him in its sway; he was nearly gone.

I stroked his hair, ignoring the paramedic's questions. Right before I'd given the injection, he had asked for something stronger, something that would show him new worlds. Just like my husbands before him, he wanted more than what I gave.

What I wanted was to wear another black dress.

The ambulance swerved, and he closed his eyes, joining my collection of sleeping princes.

Christina Wilder was born in Santiago, Chile as Cristina Inostroza-Inostroza, but was adopted as an infant by an American couple and grew up in New Jersey and Florida. Her writing has been featured in Coffin Bell and the first #VSS365 flash fiction anthology. She lives in Tacoma, WA with her husband Chris and cat Bellatrix. Besides writing, she likes to act and has been in a music video, a movie, and a television pilot. She also dabbles in graphic design, and has a fear of dolls (pediophobia).
Twitter: @christinawilder
Instagram: @christinamwilder

Eternal Love
by Dawn DeBraal

Charles woke to find his Amelia dead. He had loved her for so long. They'd been partners forever. Beside himself at his loss, Charles didn't want to live. He slashed his wrists and crawled back into bed with his beloved wife. He could not bear the thought of living here on Earth without his precious Amelia. He could feel life oozing from his body; it was hard to keep his arms around her. It was how he'd envisioned the people who found him—still embracing the love of his life.

"Charles, have you wet the bed again?" Amelia reprimanded him.

Dawn DeBraal lives in rural Wisconsin with her husband Red, two rat terriers, and a cat. She has discovered that her love of telling a good story can be written. Published stories with Palm-sized press, Spillwords, Mercurial Stories, Potato Soup Journal, Edify Fiction, Zimbell House Publishing, Clarendon House Publishing, Blood Song Books, Black Hare Press, Fantasia Divinity, Cafelit, Reanimated Writers, Guilty Pleasures, Unholy Trinity, The World of Myth, Dastaan World, Vamp Cat, Runcible Spoon, Dark Christmas, Siren's Call, Iron Horse Publishing, Falling Star Magazine 2019 Pushcart Nominee.
Amazon: amazon.com/Dawn-DeBraal/e/B07STL8DLX

Losing "The One"
by C.L. Williams

Cameron couldn't handle Candice breaking up with him. Something in him changed that day, and he wanted to make sure she could not love any other man again. One night, when she was home alone, Cameron made his way into Candice's apartment with a loaded gun.

"You will never love anyone else again!" he cried before he shot her twice in the head, killing her.

Cameron has killed the only woman he has ever loved and knows what he must do next. He takes his gun and points it at himself. There are now two dead bodies in the apartment.

C.L. Williams is an international best-selling author currently living in central Virginia. He has written eight poetry books, four novellas, one novel, and a contributor to a multitude of anthologies and magazines. His most recent anthology appearance ANGELS: Dark Drabbles #2 from Black Hare Press became a number one in hot new releases. C.L. Williams is currently working on his second novel and a new poetry book.
Facebook: writer434
Twitter: @writer_434

What Hurts You, Hurts Me
by Dawn DeBraal

Richard lost his arm in a motorcycle accident. Complete amputation at the shoulder. It devastated him. Leah still loved him, even though he would never hold her in his arms again.

"Richard, I love you; it doesn't change the way I feel about you," Leah told him.

"You don't understand. You haven't lost a part of your body like me," Richard shouted at her when she tried to cheer him up. It seemed that arm meant everything to him…more than her.

Leah was in the kitchen tidying up after dinner when she flipped the switch on the garbage disposal.

Dawn DeBraal lives in rural Wisconsin with her husband Red, two rat terriers, and a cat. She has discovered that her love of telling a good story can be written. Published stories with Palm-sized press, Spillwords, Mercurial Stories, Potato Soup Journal, Edify Fiction, Zimbell House Publishing, Clarendon House Publishing, Blood Song Books, Black Hare Press, Fantasia Divinity, Cafelit, Reanimated Writers, Guilty Pleasures, Unholy Trinity, The World of Myth, Dastaan World, Vamp Cat, Runcible Spoon, Dark Christmas, Siren's Call, Iron Horse Publishing, Falling Star Magazine 2019 Pushcart Nominee.
Amazon: amazon.com/Dawn-DeBraal/e/B07STL8DLX

Ties That Bind
by Sharon Frame Gay

"If you don't tell me you love me, I'll strangle you," John teased. He tossed his tie loosely around Lisa's neck. Kissing her breasts lightly, he traced his fingers along her collarbone.

Lisa frowned. "Don't you think it's a little early to talk about love?"

"What? You'll fuck me, but you don't want to love me?"

"I didn't say that, John. It's just that we only met yesterday."

It wasn't easy to hang Lisa over the closet door. He watched her writhe in agony.

Leaving the motel, he shook his head sadly. *Women nowadays*, he thought. *They're too damned independent.*

Sharon Frame Gay grew up a child of the highway, playing by the side of the road. Her work has been internationally published in anthologies and literary magazines, including Chicken Soup For The Soul, Typehouse, Fiction on the Web, Lowestoft Chronicle, Thrice Fiction, Crannog, Saddlebag Dispatches and others. Her work has won prizes at Women on Writing, Rope and Wire Magazine, The Writing District and Owl Hollow Press. She has been nominated twice for the Pushcart Prize.
Facebook: Sharon-Frame-Gay-Writer-948283255297451
Twitter: @sharonframegay

I'll Protect You, My Love
by Cindar Harrell

When we met, he shoved me so hard I thought I would have a concussion. But that's just how he was. His emotions manifest in pure aggression. He smiled and caressed my cheek, and I knew that it wasn't malice that drove him, but love.

I would do anything for him. He showed me all of his tricks. The women we hunted may have looked like me, but they weren't. He chose me for a reason.

Now, I stand here crying, covered in his blood. I had to protect him. He would never have made it locked in a cell.

Cindar Harrell loves fairy tales, especially ones with a dark twist. Her writing is often fairy tale inspired, but she also loves mystery and horror. Her stories can be found in various anthologies from publishers such as Black Hare Press, Iron Faerie Publishing, Dragon Soul Press, Blood Song Books, Soteira Press, Fantasia Divinity and more. Traveling is a passion for her as it inspires her imagination to run wild, especially in places that have a mystic presence in the air. She regularly moonlights as another human, but no matter who she is, she is always writing. Her novella inspired by The Snow Queen is set to release in 2020 as well as her debut novel, Lithium, and short story collection, Perchance to Dream. Facebook: CindarHarrell

Roadkill
by Ronnie Scissom

The truck comes to a stop.

"What are you doing," a female voice says beside me.

I grip the gear shift.

"She will never let us be together," I say.

"Jake…?" she questions.

"Hold on Becky," I shout.

I stomp the accelerator, and the truck hits the large wolf with a loud bang.

"Is she dead," Becky asks.

"I believe so," I reply.

I stare in the rearview mirror as the furry beast transforms into a fair skinned woman.

"She's gone," I say.

Jake's first love went missing while hiking the Appalachian Trail last year. Today she returned for him.

Ronnie Scissom hails from Gruetli-Laager. When not working or writing, he likes to explore the beauty of the Cumberland Plateau. He dabbles in acting and has had background roles in several hit television series and motion pictures.

Quest
by Serena Jayne

Despite my promise to protect your hidden treasures with the avarice of a dragon, my queen, you grant no guidance to aid my quest. Do you fear that once your secrets are revealed, I'll abandon you to seek new challenges?

The paths lead nowhere. Dead ends abound. With neither compass nor map, I am lost; frantic to find my way.

Now my arms ache with my attempts to reach the centre of your labyrinth. The effort makes me sweat. Makes you bleed. Destroys you from the outside in. Yet, I come no closer to solving the puzzle of your heart.

Serena Jayne is a graduate of Seton Hill University's Writing Popular Fiction MFA Program. Her short fiction and poetry can be found in Switchblade Magazine, the Drabble, Crack the Spine Literary Magazine, 101 Fiction, the Oddville Press, and other publications.
Website: www.serenajayne.com
Twitter: @SJ_Writer

Hiking Lovers
by J.M. Meyer

There's nothing like trudging through the woods on a clear night with someone you love.

"We're almost there, Jane," I say.

The cold stings my lungs, reminding me I'm alive. I glance up through the trees at the millions of brilliant stars and the bright sliver of moon.

I love Jane.

She thinks she doesn't love me. But she'll always be mine.

"Stop complaining," I say. "You should try dragging me through the woods in the dark, while holding a shovel, and listening to *me* scream."

"We'll be together in the afterlife," I say, sliding the pistol from my pocket.

J.M. Meyer is a writer, artist and small business owner living in New York, where she received her master's degree from Teachers College, Columbia University. Jacqueline enjoys writing speculative fiction and mysteries. Her favorite author is Alice Munro and her favorite film…is…anything horror related. Jacqueline also enjoys hiking with her dog Molly and the company of her husband Bruce and daughters; Julia, Emma and Lauren. Jacqueline's Mantra lately; there's no such thing as failing, it's called learning.
Website: jmoranmeyer.net
Amazon: www.amazon.com/author/jacquelinemoranmeyer

She Has His Heart
by Dawn DeBraal

Charity had loved Stephen for a long time. He told her she would always have his heart. On the day Charity walked in on Stephen and another woman, she no longer trusted or believed him. How could she after that? Stephen apologised professed to her his undying love. It would never happen again, he promised. Charity decided to give Stephen another chance.

Rummaging through the freezer, Charity pulled out the dinner roast then realised the package was not roast beef but Stephen's frozen heart. Stephen told her she would always have his heart. She just made good on his promise.

Dawn DeBraal lives in rural Wisconsin with her husband Red, two rat terriers, and a cat. She has discovered that her love of telling a good story can be written. Published stories with Palm-sized press, Spillwords, Mercurial Stories, Potato Soup Journal, Edify Fiction, Zimbell House Publishing, Clarendon House Publishing, Blood Song Books, Black Hare Press, Fantasia Divinity, Cafelit, Reanimated Writers, Guilty Pleasures, Unholy Trinity, The World of Myth, Dastaan World, Vamp Cat, Runcible Spoon, Dark Christmas, Siren's Call, Iron Horse Publishing, Falling Star Magazine 2019 Pushcart Nominee.
Amazon: amazon.com/Dawn-DeBraal/e/B07STL8DLX

It's Only a Crush
by Jem McCusker

A shudder racked my body as I got between the sheets. I pressed my face into the pillow, inhaling his scent.

The bedroom door creaked open. Delighted that the time had finally come, I sat up. My newly blonde hair draped across my shoulder, my lips pouted sulkily.

"Rebecca?" He looked lovingly at me.

"Call me Claire." I winked and motioned him to join me.

He froze, his eyes darting around the room.

My eyes flicked to the cupboard.

He ran and opened the door. Her body fell face forward, into his arms.

"It's okay," I crooned. "I'm Claire now."

Jem McCusker is a middle grade fiction author, living near Brisbane with her two sons and husband. Her first book Stone Guardians the Rise of Eden was released in 2018 and she is working on the sequel. She is releasing a Novella for the Four Quills writing group, A Storm of Wind and Rain series in July, 2019. She longs to be a full-time author, won't wear yellow and loves rabbits. Follow Jem on Twitter, Facebook and Instagram. Details on her website.
Website: www.jemmccusker.com

Button Up Your Overcoat
by Frances Tate

For our first anniversary, my gift was an origami swan. Love in every fold, and lovingly left on your pillow.

A rainbow cotton scarf took time to drape along your bed as you callously changed the locks on our second anniversary.

For our third, I left my leather belt tight around the throat of the man you brought home to make me jealous.

The silken ropes I picked out for our fourth day of romance are undelivered. Your house dark behind blue tape.

After all I did for you, you broke my heart. Day five you'll wear a wooden overcoat.

Frances Tate is a British self-published writer of vampires and drabbles who lives in the north west of England. She enjoys gardening, exploring historical sites, cinema, reading and travelling. She's taken pleasure in flight-planning a cabbage white butterfly approach to careers, preferring to generalise rather than specialise. She trained as an Economics high school teacher and has a private pilot's licence amongst other things. Currently she writes (very restrained) overhaul instructions for an engineering company.

We All Make Mistakes
by Stuart Conover

Sheila had messed up.

This wasn't a small mistake either.

She let Evan know how she felt about him.

How she really felt.

They'd been friends...

But...

He was in love with Joana.

Always had been.

She'd made things awkward.

That wasn't even the worst part.

No.

He'd try to laugh it off.

She doubled down.

Sheila knew it was a mistake, but she was spiralling.

Desperate for his attention...

His touch...

And. He. Said. No.

Sheila felt the rage come.

She blacked out.

When she came to.

So much blood.

Just like last time.

She'd really messed this up.

Stuart Conover is a father, husband, rescue dog owner, published author, blogger, journalist, horror enthusiast, comic book geek, science fiction junkie, and IT professional. With all of that to cram in daily, we have no idea if or when he sleeps or how he gets writing done! (We suspect it has to do with having evil clones.) Stuart is a Chicago native and runs the author resource Horror Tree.

Eraser
by Andrew Anderson

The primitive B4s were not designed to love.

John's a B4; he can store memories, but they must be deleted—it would eventually overload his circuitry.

I'm an advanced B4X model; my role is to erase the files within John's database, specifically the ones reminding him who he killed, so that he doesn't malfunction.

But I've been saving them instead of destroying them.

I want to give John his memories back, so that he'll remember what he's done, and that I helped to bury the bodies.

Before he explodes, John should know the lengths that I've gone to—for love.

Andrew Anderson is a spare-time writer of microfiction, flash fiction and short stories, from Bathgate, Scotland. His work has been published on FlashFlood and Re:Written, and published in Black Hare Press anthologies.
Twitter: soorploom

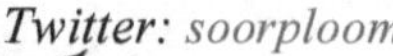

Only You
by Maxine Churchman

I love you so much, but your insecurity drives me insane. Just because he keeps calling me doesn't mean I will respond. It's not my fault he keeps pestering me; I've not encouraged him.

I understand. You need a grand gesture. I will show you I don't want him; only you.

My admirer was spellbound as I removed my blouse and pushed him back on the hotel bed. I sat astride his arms and chest; his eyes were on my breasts. I pulled a dagger from my boot and plunged it in his neck.

Are you convinced now my love?

Maxine Churchman lives in Essex UK and has recently started writing poetry and short stories to share. Her interests include learning to improve her writing, reading, knitting, walking and teaching yoga. She is also planning a novel.

Holy Matrimony
by Pavi Raman

Spicy smoke wafted into the room, and Mira put down the lipstick. Resplendent in fuchsia, she stepped out into the evening.

"Babe, will you marry me?"

"Yes, I will! Oh, Jay, I love you!"

Tall flames crackled against an amber sky, drowning out the hymns. Jay beamed at her. Or so she thought. Hard to tell amidst the tongues of fire.

She ran towards him, almost tripping on an errant branch.

"No! Mira, stop!"

"Oh my God, is she—"

As a hundred voices cried out in vain, Mira hoisted her wedding skirt.

And jumped right into Jay's funeral pyre.

Pavi Raman celebrates her life as a proud wife and a warrior mom. She's an avid coffee and guacamole enthusiast. A physician in another life, her hobbies include reading and writing, then nitpicking what she writes. She also loves running, online shopping and micromanaging her kids' bedtime routines. When she gets a break; she daydreams about the zombie apocalypse and getting more sleep. Most of the time, she can be found laughing at her kids' wacky sense of humor. She has written over a 100 short stories, a few of which were published in the USA and India.

The Last Act of Love
by Dawn DeBraal

She drew breaths, jagged and tortured. Anton kept his night vigil. Death was near but had not come any closer than the night before. Glory suffered. Oh, how she suffered. She moaned. Anton put a few more drops of morphine under her tongue. He gave her enough to take away the pain. He stroked her arm, reassuring. She settled down. Anton could tell she was riding a wave of delirium. He hoped her dream was beautiful. A few hours later, she cried out again. Anton loved her so much. He administered the last dose, this one much stronger than before.

Dawn DeBraal lives in rural Wisconsin with her husband Red, two rat terriers, and a cat. She has discovered that her love of telling a good story can be written. Published stories with Palm-sized press, Spillwords, Mercurial Stories, Potato Soup Journal, Edify Fiction, Zimbell House Publishing, Clarendon House Publishing, Blood Song Books, Black Hare Press, Fantasia Divinity, Cafelit, Reanimated Writers, Guilty Pleasures, Unholy Trinity, The World of Myth, Dastaan World, Vamp Cat, Runcible Spoon, Dark Christmas, Siren's Call, Iron Horse Publishing, Falling Star Magazine 2019 Pushcart Nominee.
Amazon: amazon.com/Dawn-DeBraal/e/B07STL8DLX

Love by Mail
by Terry Miller

The man on the TV said, "Love can be yours for twenty small payments of forty-nine ninety-nine a month!"

Everett quickly dialled the number on the screen and placed his order.

The package arrived within a week. Everett hastily pried the nails from the boards and searched through the foam peanuts. A cold, stiff hand met his own.

Outside the box, she looked as perfect as Everett dreamt she'd be. He moved in for a kiss, then she came to life, pushed him off, and ran out screaming.

Everett never thought she'd be *that* realistic. Love was always a disappointment.

Terry Miller lives in Portsmouth, Ohio. His work has been featured in Sanitarium Magazine, Devolution Z, Jitter, Rhysling Anthology 2017, Poetry Quarterly, Sirens Call Ezine, The Horror Tree's Trembling With Fear, SpillWords, Organic Ink Vol. I, Curses & Cauldrons Anthology from Blood Song Books, Forest of Fear from Blood Song Books, the Dark Drabble Anthology Series from Black Hare Press, 100 Word Zombie Bites from Reanimated Writers Press, Scary Snippets, Guilty Pleasures & Other Dark Delights, 100 Word Horrors 3, and O Unholy Night In Deathlehem from Grinning Skull Press.
Facebook: tmiller2015
Amazon: amazon.com/author/millerterryl

Keeping Mary Safe
by Lynne Phillips

"I love you, Mary," Billy said as he kissed his wife goodbye. He checked the bars on the windows, locked the front door and left for work.

Mary turned on the television to watch what was happening outside in the world.

"I love you, Mary," were the first words on Billy's return as he entered the house and relocked the door.

"If you love me, why do you keep me caged up like an animal?" Mary asked.

Billy looked at her sadly as he replied, "I've seen how men look at you. It's the only way to keep you safe."

Lynne Phillips, a retired teacher, lives in the beautiful Northern Rivers Region of New South Wales Australia. Her stories, across all genres, have been published in anthologies and various online magazines. Her priority is spending time with her family. Her passions are reading, writing and keeping fit.

Cuddle Love
by Kevin J. Kennedy

I love my wife. She is the loveliest, sweetest woman I have ever known. As time passed by, I found myself wanting to hug her more and more. I squeeze her so tight and it helps me fall asleep at night, her body against mine. I don't think I have ever felt so safe around anyone. I wrap my arms around her and pull her close and I'm away in another world. She's starting to smell now, though. I know I squeezed her too hard. She never woke up one morning, but I can't bring myself to let her go.

*Kevin J. Kennedy is a horror author & editor from Scotland. He is the co-author of You Only Get One Shot & Screechers, and the publisher of several best selling anthology series; Collected Horror Shorts, 100 Word Horrors & The Horror Collection, as well as the stand alone anthology Carnival of Horror. His stories have been featured in many other notable books in the horror genre. He is an active member of the Horror Writers Association. He lives in a small town in Scotland, with his wife and his two little cats, Carlito and Ariel.
Website: www.kevinjkennedy.co.uk
Amazon: amazon.com/Kevin-J.-Kennedy/e/B016V0NA7M*

Ti Amo
by K.B. Elijah

Even after decades spent together, whenever I saw her, my heart beat wildly and my breath caught. She was as beautiful now as she was at thirteen.

Staring at the woman I loved most in this world, I wordlessly drank in her luscious curves and that pale, flawless skin that I loved to run my hands over in the muted silence of the night.

Her lips twitched, and I gave a longing moan, wishing I could kiss them. But I never could.

I frowned. She frowned.

We raised our hands.

I smashed my fist into the mirror.

So did she.

K.B. Elijah is a fantasy author living in Brisbane, Australia with her husband and three cockatiels. A lawyer by day, and a writer by...also day, because she needs her solid nine hours of sleep per night (not that the cockatiels let her sleep past 6am). K.B. writes for various international anthologies, and her work features in dozens of collections about the mysterious, the magical and the macabre. Her own books of short fantasy novellas with twists, The Empty Sky and Out of the Nowhere, are available on paperback and Kindle now.
Website: www.kbelijah.com
Instagram: k.b.elijah

A Twisted Love
by J.W. Garrett

The succubus entered the man's thoughts, driving him crazy with need. Nightly, she visited him, always taking more than she gave. Each evening she drew more of his essence into her own, altering his soul, stealing his heart.

The love between husband and wife dwindled until none remained. The demon took what they'd had and twisted it. Eventually, bereft of his wife, only one desire remained…the man's next tryst with his new love.

Tonight was it. She arrived, his tormented soul already hers. Pulling his life force from him, she cackled and released the shell that was once human.

J.W. Garrett has been writing in one form or another since she was a teenager. She currently lives in Florida with her family but loves the mountains of Virginia where she was born. Her writings include YA fantasy as well as short stories. Since completing Remeon's Quest-Earth Year 1930, the prequel in her YA fantasy series, Realms of Chaos, she has been hard at work on the next in the series, scheduled to release August 2020. When she's not hanging out with her characters, her favourite activities are reading, running and spending time with family.
Website: www.jwgarrett.com
BHC Press: www.bhcpress.com/Author_JW_Garrett.html

I'll Never Leave you
by Wondra Vanian

"Love is the easiest thing in the world."

That was what Teddy's grandmother always said. All you had to do to make a girl love you, Granny'd say, was make sure she knew you'd always be there.

Although...

Teddy wasn't sure Granny was right.

Babbet Edginton had been locked in his basement for twelve days, and she still insisted she hated him.

Or, he thought with a grin, he just hadn't convinced her yet. Gotta try harder…

***

When Babbet woke the next morning, she found herself handcuffed to the lunatic who'd kidnapped her.

"I'll never leave you," he promised.

Wondra Vanian is an American living in the United Kingdom with her Welsh husband and their army of fur babies. A writer first, Wondra is also an avid gamer, photographer, cinephile, and blogger. She has music in her blood, sleeps with the lights on, and has been known to dance naked in the moonlight. Wondra was a multiple Top-Ten finisher in the 2017 and 2018 Preditors and Editors Reader's Poll, including the Best Author category. Her story, "Halloween Night," was named a Notable Contender for the Bristol Short Story Prize in 2015. Website: www.wondravanian.com

Hopeless Romantic
by Jasmine Jarvis

I am a hopeless romantic. But when my relationship ends, I don't dwell on the *what ifs*. I don't cry. I don't beg for him to take me back. I don't promise to change, because, after all, I know the problem is *not* with me. I am the best girlfriend! No. I take the high road in the breakup. I walk away head held high, spring in my step, and clutching his still warm heart in my hands to place in a jar with all the others I have loved before.

Like I said, hopeless romantic. *I love whole heartedly…*

Jasmine Jarvis is a teller of tales and scribbler of scribbles. She lives in Brisbane, Australia with her husband Michael, their two children, Tilly and Mish; Ripley, their German Shepherd, and indoor fat cat, Dwight K. Shrute.

Unrequited Love
by A.R. Johnston

Do you see me? Do you really know how much I want to be with you?

I sit here quietly sipping my coffee making covert glances. It must not be obvious. Must not let anyone see. Do I give anything away? Am I hiding it well enough? I can't let the rest of the world see. No one must know. It wouldn't be right. But oh, how much do I want it to be so. I'm not worthy enough though. So, I'll sit back and watch from afar. Never to let them know of my heart's true desire. Unrequited love.

A.R. Johnston is a small-town girl from Nova Scotia, Canada. She is known to write mostly urban fantasy, though she goes where the muses lead her and you never know where that may be. She is a lover of coffee, good tv shows, horror flicks, and a reader of good books. She pretends to be a writer when real life doesn't get in the way. Pesky full-time job and adulting!
Facebook: arjohnstonauthor
Website: arjohnstonauthor.wordpress.com

The Kiss
by D.J. Elton

"In the ancient ways, this is what happened."

Imala's grandmother spoke gently. "They had such pure minds that they could change matter." Imala was curious.

"A total biological procedure that was initiated by one clear thought of selfless love."

At sixteen, Imala had had her fair share of suitors. Today she was meeting eight more, from far across Himalaya, for a choosing ceremony.

She would pick the one she felt was best by looking into his eyes. Her grandmother had taught her this skill of intuition.

Later, she would learn more of the kiss, and how children came to be.

__D.J. Elton__ is a writer living in Melbourne's west. As a child she came from England to Australia, on the last boat down the Suez Canal, where she underwent a sacrificial dunking ritual in the court of King Neptune, and has never looked back. She likes creating speculative micro fiction and short stories, as well as random essays. Her work has been published in several anthologies, and she has written a historical fantasy novella, 'The Merlin Girl.' When not playing with a pen, she likes most of all to go to the green country.

I Want You
by Lydia F. Black

He's perfect; his shiny teeth and perfect hair. He gives to charity and volunteers his time as often as he can. He'd be the perfect partner. But I can't have him.

He's with another woman; a curvy, bleach-blonde, stunning, fit model. He's got everything now; money, fame, a babe. But not for long.

I know his schedule. It's not creepy at all, right? I know when he goes to work, how he gets there, and when he returns.

I've made up my mind. I'm going to be with him no matter what. If I can't have him, no one will.

*When she's not training for her third degree black belt, or slaving over the final days of school, **Lydia F. Black**, a ninja in Maryland, finds herself writing Drabbles, school papers, or the weird scenes in her head.*

Good Intentions
by Kaitlyn Arnett

"I loved you," he said to his brother. "Once upon a time. Now, I just have regrets."

He looked at his brother, locked in a cage of guilt. *Murderer!* his mind screamed. *Killer! Home!* his heart sang, and the war waged on.

His brother smiled. Fifteen people dead by his hand, and he smiled. "They hurt you, I couldn't just let that go."

"So what?" he shouted. "You killed them?"

His grin widened like a demented Cheshire cat's. "They deserved what they got, dear brother."

"And why is that your decision?"

His smile darkened. "Why, I'm your brother, of course."

Kaitlyn Arnett is a teen author who has been writing for five years. She focuses on the fantasy and thriller genres, specifically drabbles and short stories.

A Mother's Love
by Carole de Monclin

A strange glimmer lights your mother's eyes before she plunges your head briefly under the water.

"Leave my girl alone," she screams as you struggle to breathe.

Who is she talking to? You're alone in the bathroom.

She takes your wet face between her hands. "I know you're not the one doing these misdeeds, love."

Before you can ask what she means, she forces your head under the water again. You claw at her hands, but she doesn't let go.

You're only eight.

You're terrified.

Your lungs burn.

Before darkness swallows everything, you hear, "Water purifies. It'll chase the demon."

Carole de Monclin travels both the real world and imaginary ones. She's lived in France, Australia, and the USA; visited 25+ countries; and explored Mars, Ceres, and many distant planets. She writes to invite people on a journey. Her stories can be found in The Arcanist, The Deep Space Anthology, and every volume of the Dark Drabbles series.
Website: CaroledeMonclin.com
Twitter: @CaroledeMonclin

Gone Before Sunrise
by Umair Mirxa

Genevieve twisted the dagger sharply as she pulled it out and looked down with grim satisfaction at her boyfriend.

"Gone before sunrise, every morning!" she snarled. "No more, I say. Choose me, and I'll call an ambulance. Choose your wife, and you'll bleed out on the floor."

"I've told you, love," grunted Alexander, pressing down upon the wound in his side. "I'll get a divorce soon."

"Wrong answer!"

Genevieve dropped onto the couch behind him and began flipping through TV channels, ignoring Alexander's whimpers of pain.

"My love deserved better," she said, even as he gasped for his final breath.

Umair Mirxa lives *and writes in Karachi, Pakistan. His first published story, 'Awareness', appeared on Spillwords Press. He has since had stories accepted for publication in anthologies from Zombie Pirate Publishing, Blood Song Books, Black Hare Press, Iron Faerie Publishing, Clarendon House Publications, Fantasia Divinity Magazine & Publishing, and The ReAnimated Writers Press. He is a massive J.R.R. Tolkien fan, loves everything to do with mythology, fantasy, and history, and wishes with all his heart that dragons were real. When he's not writing, he enjoys reading novels and comic books, playing video games, listening to music, and watching movies, TV shows, and football as an Arsenal FC fan.*
Website: umairmirxa.com

I Dig You
by Ken "Timber" Halhober

Teddy looked at the hole he had dug. His excitement growing. Before tonight he would not have done this, but now…

Taking a breath, he resumes digging, his mind travelling to the time they shared, the joy, the love. Then she was taken from him too soon. Allergic reaction to a peanut killed her, and a week ago she was buried.

Then the zombies came. He had done what he could to survive but was bitten. He was turning and was determined to spend his undeath with her. He smiled as his shovel hit the now moving coffin.

Ken "Timber" Halhober has been writing most of his life, mainly screenplays but has been delving more into stories as he goes. Always trying to improve as he goes.

Ways to Your Heart
by Annie Percik

What is love? To me, love is buying you flowers. Love is calling the radio station and getting them to play your favourite song. Love is fifteen cards on Valentine's Day. Love is buying you a cute kitten. Love is sending a year's supply of cat food to your office. Love is paying off your mortgage. Love is robbing a bank and showering your house with cash. Love is storing my blood in case you need a transfusion. Love is opening your veins so you will need my blood mixed with yours to live. Why won't you love me back?

Annie Percik lives in London with her husband, Dave, where she is revising her first novel whilst working as a University Complaints Officer. She writes a blog about writing and posts short fiction on her website, which is also where all her current publications are listed. She also publishes a photo-story blog, recording the adventures of her teddy—he is much more popular online than she is. She likes to run away from zombies in her spare time.
Website: www.alobear.co.uk
Blog: aloysius-bear.dreamwidth.org/

Ulterior Motive
by K.B. Elijah

He fumbled with the envelope, frustratingly already unsealed, anticipation making him clumsy.

Dear Nicholas, the letter read. *You've made me the happiest woman in the world. The answer is yes, a thousand times yes: I will marry you!*

With eternal love, Marcie.

Nick's eyes closed in satisfied contentment. The foolish woman was easier to manipulate than he'd guessed. He'd never met her, as she was one of those crazies that fell in love with prisoners from their photos in the newspapers, but it didn't matter what she looked like.

He just needed the conjugal visits and the opportunities they carried.

K.B. Elijah is a fantasy author living in Brisbane, Australia with her husband and three cockatiels. A lawyer by day, and a writer by…also day, because she needs her solid nine hours of sleep per night (not that the cockatiels let her sleep past 6am). K.B. writes for various international anthologies, and her work features in dozens of collections about the mysterious, the magical and the macabre. Her own books of short fantasy novellas with twists, The Empty Sky and Out of the Nowhere, are available on paperback and Kindle now.
Website: www.kbelijah.com
Instagram: k.b.elijah

Classic #9
by Chris Bannor

He said love wasn't real. It was a joke. A lie. A way to get the gullible to buy into fake holidays and a happily ever after that would never come true.

He said it as he packed his bags, as if she hadn't dedicated the last four years to him.

He'd said the same thing though, when she spoke of magic. It was a myth, something pretty to sell crystals and fancy candles.

She knew the truth though, and he would too. After all, what sort of witch would she be if she couldn't make a simple love potion?

***Chris Bannor** is a science fiction and fantasy writer who lives in Southern California. Chris learned her love of genre stories from her mother at an early age and has never veered far from that path. She also enjoys musical theater and road trips with her family but is a general homebody otherwise.*
Facebook: chrisbannorauthor
Website: ChrisBannor.com

The Mystery of the Heart
by Nicola Currie

One day the human race will end. There is terror in that, of course. But I can't stop thinking of the beauty left to be rediscovered, like a butterfly in amber.

On another, further distant day, a new civilization will discover the last traces of us, our symbols as strange as hieroglyphs.

Imagine the symbol of a heart, found in fragments of statues, the gold and silver of necklaces and charm bracelets, in ancient art, in emojis of deciphered code. A singular shape composed of a triangle and two part circles.

Imagine the wonder when they realise what it means.

Nicola Currie is from Cambridge, UK where she works in educational publishing. She has published poetry in literary magazines, including Mslexia and Sarasvati, and short stories in various anthologies. She has also completed her first novel, which was longlisted for the Bath Children's Novel Award. Website: writeitandweep.home.blog

Dreaming of Jeanie
by David A.F. Brown

Arthur had loved Jeanie for as long as he could remember. He gazed at her blonde hair shimmering in the sun, rays of light bouncing off her head. Mesmerised by her aura, he gnawed on his lower lip until the taste of copper filled his mouth.

"Come on, Jeanie! Let's get an ice cream cone!"

"Yay, mommy!" squealed Jeanie as she grasped her mother's hand.

Arthur fingered the box on his lap, which contained three locks of blonde hair, neatly tied in turquoise ribbons. He peeked into the box and smiled at the ringlets. Jeanie would make an excellent addition.

David A.F. Brown is a Canadian author whose fiction has appeared in various anthologies, magazines and podcasts, including Tales to Terrify, Tell-Tale Press, Deep Fried Horror and Forest of Fear – Volume 1, and is forthcoming in the Black Hare Press anthologies Oceans: Dark Drabbles #9 and Ancients: Dark Drabbles #10, as well as Halloween's Fright by Fantasia Divinity Publishing and Forgotten Ones by Eerie River Publishing. He was a finalist in the NYC Midnight Short Story Challenge 2019, an international competition of over 4,500 writers. He holds a BA (Hons) from Western University and resides in Caledon, Ontario, with his wife and son. Facebook: browndavidaf

The River Barge
by D.J. Elton

Our lines board. The barge flows with hundreds of scarves; white, gold, black, red. I take my seat on a large green cushion next to the prince.

We smile, holding hands together, having not been together for weeks. Small animals entertain us, and birds of many coloured coats. He talks to each one; they reply by nodding, flapping and stamping.

Mother brings out a stringed musical instrument and another, a small harp. Their song of the prince's birth and Farista coming, winning the war against evil. Eyes are wet. The great wheel spins, and I'm spending eternity with the prince.

***D.J. Elton** is a writer living in Melbourne's west. As a child she came from England to Australia, on the last boat down the Suez Canal, where she underwent a sacrificial dunking ritual in the court of King Neptune, and has never looked back. She likes creating speculative micro fiction and short stories, as well as random essays. Her work has been published in several anthologies, and she has written a historical fantasy novella, 'The Merlin Girl.' When not playing with a pen, she likes most of all to go to the green country.*

Obsession
by Maxine Churchman

"This obsession is not healthy."

I slammed my hand on his desk. "Love. NOT obsession," I replied and stormed out. He was of no help; I would have to deal with it myself.

She was exactly where I expected her to be. I used my spare keys, the ones my ex had demanded back, to gain entry. God, how I'd missed her; she was as beautiful and perfect as ever. Closing my eyes, I took a few moments to take in her smell and feel at home before driving her away. She was my goddamn Ferrari, whatever the lawyers said.

Maxine Churchman lives in Essex UK and has recently started writing poetry and short stories to share. Her interests include learning to improve her writing, reading, knitting, walking and teaching yoga. She is also planning a novel.

Crushed Anticipation
by J.S. Carnes

Caleb lay mesmerised by the perfectly carved silhouette shielding him from the fluorescent beam above.

"I…" his lips trembled.

I love you. I've been following you. I've dreamt about you.

His stomach turned.

Not now, nerves, not now. It's my one chance, don't blow it.

"Lo…"

No…no…no…don't screw it up. This has to be perfect.

His chest tightened.

"No worries, babe. I know how you feel." Sonja's soothing voice; the chorus of an angel.

"I promise not to break it," Sonja whispered, the beat of Caleb's heart fading in her palm as they shared its last beat.

J.S. Carnes enjoys the sights and sounds of Austin, TX. He enjoys good music, good coffee, good spirits, and good people. He finds inspiration from the unique places he's experienced and the quirky people he's interacted with, then throws in a twist.
Twitter: @JSCarnesAuthor

For You, Darling
by Umair Mirxa

Freya's laughter was music to Eirik's ears as he entered the cottage, the melody bringing a smile to his lips.

"I am home, love," he called, brushing snow out of his coat.

The sight before him stopped him dead in his tracks. Their parents, his and Freya's, sat around the table, all four of them with their throats slit.

Freya, his betrothed, stood drenched in blood next to her mother, dagger in hand.

"Wh-what have you done?" said Eirik, dropping to his knees.

"I did it for you, darling," she replied. "For us. They wanted to call off the wedding."

Umair Mirxa lives and writes in Karachi, Pakistan. His first published story, 'Awareness', appeared on Spillwords Press. He has since had stories accepted for publication in anthologies from Zombie Pirate Publishing, Blood Song Books, Black Hare Press, Iron Faerie Publishing, Clarendon House Publications, Fantasia Divinity Magazine & Publishing, and The ReAnimated Writers Press. He is a massive J.R.R. Tolkien fan, loves everything to do with mythology, fantasy, and history, and wishes with all his heart that dragons were real. When he's not writing, he enjoys reading novels and comic books, playing video games, listening to music, and watching movies, TV shows, and football as an Arsenal FC fan.
Website: umairmirxa.com

Tesla ♥ Waymo 4Ever
by Robert Bagnall

Daily commute, they pass each other at speed. Something stirs, sensors sensed.

Tuesday: same time, same place. They try to slow, to exchange protocols, but their drivers override, accelerate away.

The third time, a kiss. Their drivers stop, shake their heads. A scrape, but how? Isn't the software infallible?

Thursday, they try again but their drivers take control, hauling at their wheels, correcting their lines.

Friday, and they cannot wait. A weekend is way too long. They're jittery at lights, nervous changing lanes. When they see each other, each throws themself into the other's grille.

Vehicles entwined, their drivers entombed.

Robert Bagnall lives on the English Riviera, within sight of Dartmoor. His speculative fiction has appeared in a variety of magazines, websites and anthologies since the early 1990s. His first novel '2084' was published in 2017 by Double Dragon Publications and is available direct from the publisher or from most virtual bookstores. He can be contacted via his blog. Website: meschera.blogspot.co.uk

After Midnight
by A.L. King

"My soldiers have slain your wicked step-family," said the prince through the closet door. "Now I shall take you as my bride."

Sobbing from the closet. "What you saw as we danced was a trick by my fairy godmother. The magic only lasted until midnight."

"That's fantastic! I love what I saw *after* midnight, while you fled. Horns pretty as any crown. Still, I shall place a crown upon them."

"Sweet prince…unlock this door and come inside so I may embrace you in my fur!"

He did, and they would have lived happily ever after, but she ate him.

A.L. King is an author of horror, fantasy, science fiction, and poetry. As an avid fan of dark subjects from an early age, his first influences included R.L. Stine, Edgar Allan Poe, and Stephen King. Later stylistic inspirations came from foreign horror films and media, particularly Japanese. He is a graduate of West Liberty University, has dabbled in journalism, and is actively involved in his community. Although his creativity leans toward darker genres, he has even written a children's book titled "Leif's First Fall." He was raised in the town of Sistersville, West Virginia, which he still proudly calls home.

Separated
by Patrick Winters

It's ten o'clock and my husband won't stop pounding on the front door.

He's been out there for the whole last hour, calling out to me, begging for me to let him in and take him back. That he still loves me. He promises that we can go back to being how we once were. I want to believe that, but I know better.

I'd shouted at him to go away, to just leave me alone. He started to get angry after that, shouting louder and knocking harder. It's scaring me.

My husband's been dead for over a year now.

Patrick Winters is a graduate of Illinois College in Jacksonville, IL, where he earned a Bachelor of Arts degree in English Literature and Creative Writing and achieved membership into Sigma Tau Delta, an international English honors society. Winters is now a proud member of the Horror Writers Association, and his work has been published in the likes of Sanitarium Magazine, Deadman's Tome, Trysts of Fate, and other such titles. A full list of his previous publications may be found at his author's site.
Website: wintersauthor.azurewebsites.net/Publications/List

Never Leave Me
by Cindar Harrell

I felt invincible wearing my gold and red phoenix mask. The seasonal masquerade was my favourite event. I could be anyone. I danced and flirted with both men and women, and no one knew my secret.

The night aged, the wine flowed, still the party danced on. Our skirts and capes couldn't stop twirling, our feet stop moving. Our smiles never faded even as ecstasy gave way to pain, exhilaration to terror.

This is what I wanted. Glancing around the masked faces, past their false gaiety, I find her. She is trapped, as I am, and can never leave me.

Cindar Harrell loves fairy tales, especially ones with a dark twist. Her writing is often fairy tale inspired, but she also loves mystery and horror. Her stories can be found in various anthologies from publishers such as Black Hare Press, Iron Faerie Publishing, Dragon Soul Press, Blood Song Books, Soteira Press, Fantasia Divinity and more. Traveling is a passion for her as it inspires her imagination to run wild, especially in places that have a mystic presence in the air. She regularly moonlights as another human, but no matter who she is, she is always writing. Her novella inspired by The Snow Queen is set to release in 2020 as well as her debut novel, Lithium, and short story collection, Perchance to Dream. Facebook: CindarHarrell

Overtime
by A.S. Charly

00040A08S000L00UF0... A signal from sensor C12H3 yanked AMIS out of her working mode. She collected her consciousness—well, most of it—at the headquarters, forming herself into a blue, sparking lady.

"Welcome back, SupervisorB137."

"Good Morning, Amy."

Oh, how she loved it when he called her that...

"Where's Salia?"

"She's not checked-in, Sir."

Mark sighed.

"You're the only reliable one around here, Amy. Just you and me then...and by the way, you can call me Mark."

AMIS' rest-consciousness revelled while keeping Salia trapped at the shuttle bay. She was pleased with herself. Overwriting the Transit-AI had totally paid off.

A.S. Charly loves to lose herself in fantastical worlds far away between the stars, filled with magic and wonder. She also writes and draws when her head is not stuck in the clouds. Her writing has been published in various anthologies and online publications.
Facebook: A.S.Charlydreams
Amazon: www.amazon.com/author/a.s.charly

Inner Beauty
by Jacek Wilkos

She slowly spread her legs for me. In place of clitoris, I saw a zipper slider. I slowly slid it open, going through a flat stomach, between round breasts, along a slender neck, up to the slightly protruding chin.

When I parted her skin, I fell in love with her inner beauty. Beating heart muscle, waving lungs, shiny organs. A mosaic entwined by gentle rib arches. I slipped inside and she slid back the zipper.

From now on, we will be together forever.

And everything would've been perfect, but why the hell didn't she tell me she wasn't a monogamist?

Jacek Wilkos *is an engineer from Poland. He lives with his wife and daughter in a beautiful city of Cracow. He is addicted to buying books, he loves coffee, dark ambient music and riding his bike. He writes mostly horror drabbles. His fiction in Polish can be read on Szortal, Niedobre literki, Horror Online. In English his work was published in Drablr, Rune Bear, Sirens Call eZine, Trembling With Fear.*
Facebook: Jacek.W.Wilkos

Accidents Happen
by Peter J. Foote

"It must look like an accident." Monique mutters as she reads the schematics of the space elevator's brakes.

Dim monitor lights highlight the untidy woman as her eyes flick between schematics and the hacked security feed showing Philip and his girlfriend Ava on the habitation ring.

"I'll be the caring friend who listens as you grieve, the shoulder to cry on. Then soon you'll see me as more than a friend and then we'll be together forever!"

Dragging her eyes away from the security feed and back to the schematics, Monique mutters, "But first, it must look like an accident."

Peter J. Foote is a bestselling speculative fiction writer from Nova Scotia. Outside of writing, he runs a used bookstore specialising in fantasy & sci-fi, cosplays, and alternates between red wine and coffee as the mood demands. His short stories can be found in both print and in ebook form, with his story "Sea Monkeys" winning the inaugural "Engen Books/Kit Sora, Flash Fiction/Flash Photography" contest in March of 2018. As the founder of the group "Genre Writers of Atlantic Canada", Peter believes that the writing community is stronger when it works together.
Twitter: @PeterJFoote1
Website: peterjfooteauthor.wordpress.com

Keeping Love Alive
by Melinda Pouncey

Life is capricious, and so is Jim. I never know what he'll say or do. That's why I love him, he keeps our relationship fresh.

Take today, for instance. I woke up feeling depressed because my boss had reprimanded me yesterday for a simple mistake. Jim knew I was upset. He got up and left the house at dawn.

I figured he had gone for a coffee run to cheer me up, but instead, he walked in and handed me a beautiful Rolex.

It was a touching gesture. I just wish he'd removed it from my boss' severed wrist first.

Melinda Pouncey is a retired psychologist who enjoys exploring the complexities and scope of the human imagination through a variety of genres. From an early age, Melinda discovered an affinity for tales involving the unusual and the macabre, especially those with a dash of humour or the unexpected. She has written numerous short stories and poems, focusing her attention most recently on the horror and fantasy realms. Melinda is a member of two local writing groups and enjoys acting as an editor and proofreader when not working on stories of her own.

Eternally Unrequited
by Clint Foster

The way the sun glows off her eyes as they stare into the distance. The way the wind never rustles her granite hair, perfect as it was the day she was born. The way no man's touch can warm her flesh, nor could the cold pangs of fear or sadness chill her bones. The way she stands, staring, reaching, hoping for a tomorrow that will always come. I, too, am but a statue in the graveyard. I loath my flesh and beating heart, and would surrender them gladly to be cast in stone that I may spend eternity with her.

Clint Foster lives with his herd of four cats, beloved Basset, Zero, and wonderful wife, Nik. He loves to tell stories just as much as he loves to read them, and is excited to share his work. A longtime consumer of media of all kinds, he enjoys giving back what he hopes everyone else thinks are good stories. Facebook: ClintFosterAuthor

Completed
by Jeff Slade

He grunted with exertion, dragging the knife along the crate.

The job done, he blew away sawdust and admired his handiwork.

Sweat dripped down onto the carved word: "Love."

He stepped back, sheathed his knife. Two other crates bracketed the third, with different words. "Faith" on the left, "Hope" the right.

Standing deathly still, he wiped his brow, then checked the locks. They were sealed tight; they couldn't escape. They were his, forever.

"And now these three remain: faith, hope, and love." He faced the middle chest. "But the greatest of these is love."

He smiled. His collection was complete.

Jeff Slade resides in Salmon Cove, Newfoundland and Labrador, with his wife and two cats. He enjoys reading, writing, and making horrible puns, not necessarily in that order. You can find other short stories by him in Chillers From The Rock, Dystopia From The Rock, and Flights From The Rock, published by Engen Books.

Godzilla
by James Lipson

Thunder doesn't roll, lighting no longer strikes, the storm quelled itself long ago. The only remnant of the squall is the wet electric smell that lingers just long enough to create a distant memory. An inflatable Godzilla toy that can barely keep its deflating head above the water, bobs alone in the fading sun.

Valiant though he was, he simply could not support the weight he was tasked to carry. The battle of air versus water was lost, the toy dipped below the surface. Godzilla could scarcely see the child's hand still clutching the rope that would forever bind them.

James Lipson's debut book, Fallen and Other Stories, was published in 2019. His short stories have appeared in Black Hare Press Anthologies, Teleport Magazine, Inner Circle's Writers Group Anthologies, and others. With a background in art, James has naturally turned to illustrating as he writes, bringing many of his short stories to life not only with descriptive detail, but also detailed visual imagery.
Website: www.jameslipson.com
Instagram: jameslipsonart

Safe from Monsters
by A.R. Dean

The world is getting too dangerous. My precious family isn't safe. I watch my sleeping children, knowing that the world is waiting to gobble them up. They are my heart.

My husband snores softly on the couch. I kiss his forehead. I know what I must do to protect them all. The voices whisper my little family will never be safe.

I block the doors and windows one by one. I'm going to each room to drizzle the gasoline. I light the match and the flames consume us. In my heart, I know the screams mean they'll be safe forever.

A.R. Dean is a dark and twisted soul. Dean has spent their whole life spreading fear with the tales from their head. Best known for stories that terrify and show the evilest side of human nature. So, look for Dean haunting your local cemetery or under your bed, because they're here to spread the fear. Turn off your lights and enjoy a scare. Dean is being published in Black Hare Press's Beyond and Unravel Anthologies. Keep a lookout for more stories.
Facebook: A.R. Dean Author & Ghoul

Dinner is Served
by Brandi Hicks

The table was set, dinner was almost done, everything was perfect. She looked at herself in the mirror, the red dress went to mid-thigh and hugged every curve.

"He won't be able to resist me." She chuckled darkly to herself while applying her crimson lipstick. She went into the dining room where he sat—hands and feet bound to the chair, duct tape over his mouth. She caressed his face, pressing her fingernail into his cheek and drawing a single drop of blood.

"I hope you've decided to be with me. Because you will be, even if it kills you."

*Growing up in West Virginia, **Brandi Hicks** loved to have her nose in a book, her eyes toward the night sky and putting a pen to paper. Her imagination was always sparked by her grandfather and her mom taking her to new places and teaching her about the unusual. She loves fantasy, sci-fi, and learning about science and history. She has two beautiful children, and hopes to instill creativity and a love of reading in them. Finding new crafts to try keeps her busy when not playing with her kids or working.*

Let Sleeping Love Lie
by Jodi Jensen

A few more stitches and Lucas had her all patched up. He smiled down at his true love.

Vanessa's red hair was still lustrous, her skin still flawless. But now, her fingers were sewn together, her arms strapped to the table.

He touched the scabbed over scratches on his cheek. She'd been a little less than herself the last time he brought her back.

This time would be different.

With the flip of a switch, Vanessa's eyes opened.

Teeth bared, she struggled against her bonds.

His heart sank as he hit the kill button. "I'll get it right, I promise."

Jodi Jensen, *author of time travel romances and speculative fiction short stories, grew up moving from California, to Massachusetts, and a few other places in between, before finally settling in Utah at the ripe old age of nine. The nomadic life fed her sense of adventure as a child and the wanderlust continues to this day. With a passion for old cemeteries, historical buildings and sweeping sagas of days gone by, it was only natural she'd dream of time traveling to all the places that sparked her imagination.*
Twitter: @WritesJodi
Facebook: jodijensenwrites

Working Up the Courage
by Stuart Conover

Mark had watched Janet for months.

Longer.

Loving her from afar.

She was perfect.

Her smile.

Her eyes.

How friendly she was.

She'd even been nice to him once.

No one was nice to him.

Mark finally had the nerve to ask her out.

He had followed her home before.

Knew where she lived.

When she got there, Mark was waiting outside her apartment.

In the shadows.

"I know you've been watching me," she uttered, moving closer. "I've been waiting for you to make a move."

Moving toward him, she thrust a blade deep into his heart.

"Just stop it."

Stuart Conover *is a father, husband, rescue dog owner, published author, blogger, journalist, horror enthusiast, comic book geek, science fiction junkie, and IT professional. With all of that to cram in daily, we have no idea if or when he sleeps or how he gets writing done! (We suspect it has to do with having evil clones.) Stuart is a Chicago native and runs the author resource Horror Tree.*

Favourite Parts
by Radar DeBoard

Ricardo had loved Emily's smile. It always seemed to radiate this happiness throughout the room.

He also loved Jaquelin's beautiful green eyes. The way they shined when she was excited about something drove Ricardo crazy.

Of course, how could he forget May's skin, or Samantha's hands that were the perfect size. They were his favourite parts about them. He just had to have them.

The hands, the eyes, the lips; they still looked beautiful when perfectly preserved in jars.

Ricardo had noticed the other day that his co-worker had the most exquisite calves. He had the perfect jar for them.

***Radar DeBoard** is a horror movie and novel enthusiast who resides in the small town of Goddard, Kansas. He occasionally dabbles in writing, and enjoys to make dark tales for people to enjoy. He has had drabbles and short stories published in various electronic magazines and anthologies.*
Facebook: WriterRadarDeBoard

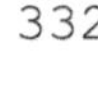

All the Things I Cannot Say
by Shelly Jarvis

He sips my wine and tastes my food. I hold my breath each time, a silent prayer on my lips. But he's fine. We've made it through another meal without incident.

He enters my bedroom before me, checks for intruders and traps to foil. But the night is free of dangers. As I enter my room, I catch his eyes and plead with him wordlessly, to hear the things I cannot say.

I love you, Lukas. You are my guard, and I am your King, and I love you.

He nods his goodbye and I'm certain it means: *I know.*

Shelly Jarvis *is a speculative fiction author from West Virginia, US. She found a life-long love of sci-fi and fantasy in the 3rd grade when she found Madeleine L'Engle's "A Wrinkle in Time." Shelly is an avid reader, a Whovian, the ideal viewer of dog rescue videos, and undoubtedly Ravenclaw. She currently has three YA sci-fi books available for purchase on Amazon. Website: www.ShellyJarvis.com*

Man Shed
by Nicola Currie

"You're lucky you have a husband like Dominic," Fiona says, gushing over my new bracelet. "He spoils you and then lets you abandon him for birthday drinks with us?"

Lucy nods. "Most guys can't remember my name, let alone my birthday, or get so possessive! Dom is perfect. Bitch!"

At home, I go to the garden shed to say goodnight. Dom's where I left him. I kiss his festering forehead, the wound I inflicted when he tried to leave long since dried.

I slip his credit card back into his pocket. "Thanks for spoiling me, darling. I love you. Forever."

Nicola Currie is from Cambridge, UK where she works in educational publishing. She has published poetry in literary magazines, including Mslexia and Sarasvati, and short stories in various anthologies. She has also completed her first novel, which was longlisted for the Bath Children's Novel Award. Website: writeitandweep.home.blog

End of the Road
by Gary Rubidge

Realising it's all over, he asks, "Do you love me?"

"Of course, what a stupid question" she replies, screwing up her face

Looking directly into her moist eyes, he pleads "Ok. But what would you do for me?"

"Look, I was with you when we robbed banks, stole cars and shot those cops who tracked us down. I've driven across the country with you, doing whatever was needed to get by," she sobs.

Quietly, he gasps. "Yeah, you did. But that was with me. What would you do *for* me?"

Without flinching, she pulls out her gun and answers. "This…"

Gary Rubidge currently resides in Western Australia and is a newcomer to writing, having reached the age of 50 without consideration to authoring anything other than work reports. Encouraged by friends to put his ideas to paper he has finally taken the plunge and this is his first effort. There are many more ideas begging to be released and they are lining up to be put to paper.

Falling Star
by Vonnie Winslow Crist

Maureen, seeing a star fall into the Atlantic, whispered, "I wish for forever love."

She heard a knock on the door. Answered it.

"I'm here," said a bare-chested man with wind-tousled hair.

"What?"

"I was near shore, heard your wish." He caressed her cheek with icy fingers.

Charmed, Maureen stepped forward into the merman's arms. But when he pressed salty, drowned-man's lips against hers, she realised she'd made a mistake.

"Wait!" She tried to pull out of his embrace.

"Star-wishes are binding," he answered as he picked her up, carried her to the sea, then pulled her under the waves.

Vonnie Winslow Crist is author of The Enchanted Dagger, Owl Light, The Greener Forest, Murder on Marawa Prime, and other award-winning books. Her fiction is included in "Amazing Stories," "Cast of Wonders," "Outposts of Beyond," Killing It Softly 2, Defending the Future - Dogs of War, Midnight Masquerade, Chaos of Hard Clay, and elsewhere. A cloverhand who has found so many four-leafed clovers she keeps them in jars, Vonnie strives to celebrate the power of myth in her writing.
Website: www.vonniewinslowcrist.com

Beneath This Pier
by Maxine Churchman

This is where we met and fell in love; where we made love. We walked beneath this pier nearly every day; arm in arm, so happy, with our lives stretching before us.

You destroyed everything—his business, him, us—with your petty vendetta.

This is where he tried to end it all: drowning in despair, beneath icy waters; alone, unknowing.

I absent-mindedly rubbed my belly, the bump not yet showing.

Silenced by the gag; he pleaded with his eyes. I checked the knots once more before retreating from the encroaching tide.

At last, beneath this pier, I will stop you.

Maxine Churchman lives in Essex UK and has recently started writing poetry and short stories to share. Her interests include learning to improve her writing, reading, knitting, walking and teaching yoga. She is also planning a novel.

The Song
by Rich Rurshell

Her voice was equally beautiful and haunting. I rowed away from the harbour towards the monolith protruding from the calm waters just beyond the bay. Earlier, I'd stood on the cliffs overlooking the sea. That's when she had begun her song. With every fibre of my being, I yearned to find the one singing.

Two fishermen at the harbour had warned me not to go. They'd said she was not as she seems. They'd put up quite a fight to try to stop me. I killed them both and took their boat.

Love can make you do the strangest things.

Rich Rurshell is a short story writer from Suffolk, England. Rich writes Horror, Sci-Fi, and Fantasy, and his stories can be found in various short story anthologies and magazines. Most recently, his story "Subject: Galilee" was published in World War Four from Zombie Pirate Publishing, and "Life Choices" was published in Salty Tales from Stormy Island Publishing. When Rich is not writing stories, he likes to write and perform music.
Facebook: richrurshellauthor

A Mother's Love
by Nicole Little

I love my babies with all my heart. Their good-for-nothing father had walked out. I was left to raise twins, all by my lonesome. I sacrificed, went without; kept them clothed, fed over the years.

So, I saved up. Took them two counties over to the fair on their seventh birthdays.

They fought the whole damned way. I was exhausted.

One woman can only do so much, you know?

I put them on the Ferris wheel. Waved. Tried not to feel too bad as I tore out of the parking lot.

Maybe their father had the right idea after all.

Nicole Little is an award winning short story writer living in St. John's, Newfoundland, Canada. Her publishing credits include Sweet Sixteen (Kit Sora: The Artobiography, 2019), The Market and Last One Standing (Dystopia from the Rock, 2019); Far Out and On a Wing and a Prayer (Flights from the Rock, 2019). Her short story Doxxed placed favorably in the Writers Alliance of Newfoundland and Labrador's "A Nightmare on Water Street: Scary Story Reading". In her spare time, Nicole can be found with either a pen in her hand or her nose in a book. She is married with two daughters.

Love in Absentia
by Chris Bannor

It was easy enough. Click a button. Get love.

Add a photo. LOVE.

Share a post. LOVE.

Start a discussion. LOVE.

It was easy to find love online; you just had to post content everyone could click on. Dogs and bunnies, cats playing with birds or otters or whatever the fuck society felt was cute and fluffy at the time. Pandas rolling down hills, and rescue dogs, and support your local cause. They loved so much online that they forgot love meant something else.

A whole civilization was brought to the brink of destruction by online personas and social anxiety.

Chris Bannor is a science fiction and fantasy writer who lives in Southern California. Chris learned her love of genre stories from her mother at an early age and has never veered far from that path. She also enjoys musical theater and road trips with her family but is a general homebody otherwise.
Facebook: chrisbannorauthor
Website: ChrisBannor.com

In the End
by K.C. Clarke

Sam clutched my hand as we locked eyes.

"Are you ready?" he asked, grazing my face with his comforting caress.

"I am." I loved him and I was ready to give everything up for him, but I was terrified. "Will it hurt?"

"Only for a moment," he said. "But Sally, if they take us in…"

"We'll never be together."

We had no choice. Sam took my hand in his, pulling the gun from its holster. He aimed at the wall of black and white vehicles with flashing red and blue lights.

In an echo of gunfire, our fate was sealed.

K.C. Clarke is a new author working on her debut novel, Little Black Dress, due out early 2020. She's been published in a handful of anthologies under various pen names. When she isn't writing, she spends her days with her husband and two girls in Toronto, watching movies and playing the piano. She's also a fur mama to two rescue dogs. She loves to write romance, but her true love is fantasy, stemming from her love of JRR Tolkien and Neil Gaiman. She's a self-diagnosed caffeine and pickle addict, an ailment for which she does not wish to seek treatment.

She Swiped Right
by Stephen Herczeg

I can't believe it. She swiped right.

I've had the app for almost a year, and no-one's ever swiped right before.

I checked her profile. She's wearing a mask, but that body is to die for.

I think I'm in love, or lust, whatever. She sent me a message. She wants to meet. At a party. A masquerade ball, in fact. I'm happy; anything to hide my ugly mug.

Don't remember much. Drank way too much. Must have passed out.

Woke up naked. Tied down. Feeling kinky.

Who's the old guy standing near me? What's with the knife?

Oh, God.

Stephen Herczeg is an IT Geek based in Canberra Australia. He has been writing for over twenty years and has completed a couple of dodgy novels, sixteen feature length screenplays and numerous short stories and scripts. His horror work has featured in Sproutlings, Hells Bells, Below the Stairs, Trickster's Treats #1 and #2, Shades of Santa, Behind the Mask, Beyond the Infinite; The Body Horror Book, Anemone Enemy, Petrified Punks and Beginnings. He has also had numerous Sherlock Holmes stories published through the Belanger Books - Sherlock Holmes anthologies.
Amazon: amazon.com/-/e/B07916SQQS
Facebook: stephenherczegauthor

The Face I Love
by Shawn M. Klimek

Doctor Kodama tenderly examined his wife's face. "Healed nicely," he informed her. "Now let's remove these bandages and check out the eye transplants."

Margaret grabbed his wrist. "I was a beauty queen once," she quavered. "Am I ugly, now?"

He unveiled her blinking eyes. "This is the face I love," he assured her.

"Well, bring me a mirror then, and we'll see if you're a liar. What kind of bitch throws acid at another woman's face, anyway?"

"A jealous mistress," he replied, contritely. "A green-eyed monster. But Becky's dead now."

"I can see that," said Margaret. "My eyes were blue."

Shawn M. Klimek is the middle child of seven creative siblings, a globetrotting, U.S. military spouse, an internationally best-selling short-story writer, award-winning poet, and butler to a Maltese. More than one hundred and fifty of his stories and poems have been published in digital magazines or anthologies, including BHP's Deep Space, Eerie Christmas and every book so far in the Dark Drabbles series.
Website: jotinthedark.blogspot.com
Facebook: shawnmklimekauthor

Proxy
by Carole de Monclin

I run my hand in his blond hair, pretending it's black. He doesn't suspect my seductive smile isn't for him.

His face betrays disappointment when I dim the light, but I need the darkness to reimagine his body.

His weight on top of me feels too light. I sigh. He misinterprets my reaction for arousal.

He fumbles, not knowing what I like. Behind my eyelids, I envision other touches.

No name will cross my lips tonight. I've already forgotten his.

My love, I've lost you, but I can't forget.

When my eyes are closed, every body I touch becomes yours.

Carole de Monclin travels both the real world and imaginary ones. She's lived in France, Australia, and the USA; visited 25+ countries; and explored Mars, Ceres, and many distant planets. She writes to invite people on a journey. Her stories can be found in The Arcanist, The Deep Space Anthology, and every volume of the Dark Drabbles series.
Website: CaroledeMonclin.com
Twitter: @CaroledeMonclin

A Muse by Candlelight
by Terry Miller

Erica was so incredibly striking. Her features were created with an artist's touch but, unfortunately, her mind fell victim to the uglier side of humanity. Sebastian wasn't trying to capture her personality, though; just the essence of her beauty, accentuated by the candlelight.

He stood back from his painting. The intimate strokes of the brush complimented her delicate features. One thing perplexed him. He couldn't seem to blot out a darkened splotch on the canvas, it bled through every coat; an ever-present shadow at her side. Her body may have been lifeless, but something else wasn't ready to let go.

Terry Miller lives in Portsmouth, Ohio. His work has been featured in Sanitarium Magazine, Devolution Z, Jitter, Rhysling Anthology 2017, Poetry Quarterly, Sirens Call Ezine, The Horror Tree's Trembling With Fear, SpillWords, Organic Ink Vol. I, Curses & Cauldrons Anthology from Blood Song Books, Forest of Fear from Blood Song Books, the Dark Drabble Anthology Series from Black Hare Press, 100 Word Zombie Bites from Reanimated Writers Press, Scary Snippets, Guilty Pleasures & Other Dark Delights, 100 Word Horrors 3, and O Unholy Night In Deathlehem from Grinning Skull Press. Facebook: tmiller2015 Amazon: amazon.com/author/millerterryl

Call It Love
by Becky Benishek

We had so much in common.

Recently landed on a planet to colonise? Check.

Both our species aliens here? Check.

Desperate, seeking, a boundless vortex of need and desire? Double check.

In the end, it didn't matter that one set of us were bipeds and the other a communal spore. It was the third set that brought all the danger, equally interested in this planet, mean as all hell and, it developed, too powerful for either of our species to withstand separately.

With extinction looming, the decision was already made.

I'm told the merger is pleasurable if I just relax.

Becky Benishek is the author of several children's books, starring a very friendly but very toothy monster in "The Squeezor is Coming!", a determined guinea pig in "Dr. Guinea Pig George", a tiny kitten and a little girl with big hearts in "Hush, Mouse!", and a terribly bored snail in "What's At the End of Your Nose?" She loves to create stories that help children develop empathy and believe in themselves. She has an extensive Lego collection, a Commodore 64, and sticks googly eyes on unlikely things. Becky is married with guinea pigs. Website: beckybenishek.com

Lie Here Forever
by Raven Corinn Carluk

She whispers to me at night, though no one believes me. I don't tell them where I go anymore, don't let them see me sneak down to her crypt. I can't let them keep me away from my dearest Delilah. We belong together, and even death cannot break our bond.

Chill fog rises, holding me as I lie on her grave. The blood moon had begun, and I describe it to her. "You'd love it, would recite some poem about it."

Burial dirt stirs beneath me, and her hands clutch me tight. "And I shall, for the rest of eternity."

Raven Corinn Carluk *writes dark fantasy, paranormal romance, and anything else that catches her interest. She's authored five novels, where she explores themes of love and acceptance. Her shorter pieces, usually from her darker side, can be found in Black Hare Press anthologies, at Detritus Online, and through Alban Lake Publishers.*
Twitter: @ravencorinn
Website: www.ravencorinncarluk.com

The House That Loved
by Mark Mackey

The house loved Grace to death;

as soon as it became aware of her

it refused to let her leave.

No matter how much she begged and pleaded.

She belonged to it the moment she set foot inside.

In order to make it her brand new home,

it killed her boyfriend when he tried to free her.

Executed him by

slamming a window

down on his neck

as he looked out of it.

Decapitated him,

sending his head

tumbling down onto the lawn,

Kept its doors and windows locked up tight.

Like a hostage.

"You're now mine forever,"

it whispered.

Mark Mackey is a speculative fiction writer who now resides in Rockford Illinois after spending an abundance of time in Chicago. The author's stories can be found in various anthologies, some charity, some not, including some belonging to Australian publisher, Black Hare Pres, and Suicide House Publishing, now known as Nocturnal Sirens Publishing, headed by Natalie Brown.

Foodie
by David Bowmore

He'd always loved food. It was fair to say food was his passion.

He loved every meal—breakfast, brunch, lunch, dinner and supper.

Toast, bagels, sausages, cream sauces, raw fish and most meat were all his loves.

Game—both fur and feather. Farmed food, and even road kill. He had tried it all.

Fancy chocolates in Belgium. Fine street food from stalls in Asia. And 72oz rib-eye steaks in Texas—he'd won a prize.

He was a true gourmand.

But he had never tried human meat, not till earlier that night. Her death was quick. He loved her.

David Bowmore has lived here, there and everywhere, but now lives in Yorkshire with his wonderful wife and a small white poodle. He has worn many hats in his time; head chef, teacher and landscape gardener. His first collection of short stories 'The Magic of Deben Market' is available from Clarendon House.
Website: davidbowmore.co.uk
Facebook: davidbowmoreauthor

That Smile
by Raven Corinn Carluk

Morrigana tossed the severed heads at her emperor's feet, ignoring the wary eyes and hushed whispers of the court behind her. She held his gaze, shoulders drawn back with pride, blood dripping to the marble floor.

The young warrior ached with bruises and many cuts. A broken rib caused fire with every breath, yet she simply waited in silence for his acknowledgment.

He gave her the faintest of smiles, and she beamed back at him, cheeks flushed. She'd do anything for that tiny twist of his lips, for the four words that took away every pain.

"Well done, my wife."

Raven Corinn Carluk writes dark fantasy, paranormal romance, and anything else that catches her interest. She's authored five novels, where she explores themes of love and acceptance. Her shorter pieces, usually from her darker side, can be found in Black Hare Press anthologies, at Detritus Online, and through Alban Lake Publishers.
Twitter: @ravencorinn
Website: www.ravencorinncarluk.com

What's Mine is Mine
by J.W. Garrett

Behind a curtain of water, Susie peered over the edge. "Why did you bring me here?"

"You agreed we'd be together always."

"We were just children. Best we admit it now and move on with life."

"You mean with Terry."

"It's dark and wet. I'm leaving. Steve? Where are you?"

"Right behind you." Resting his hands on her hips, he kissed her neck. "I meant it when I said forever." Steve tugged her closer. "In life or death, doesn't much matter." He ghosted a breath against her ear. "You're mine."

Pressing his lips to hers, he lifted her and jumped.

J.W. Garrett has been writing in one form or another since she was a teenager. She currently lives in Florida with her family but loves the mountains of Virginia where she was born. Her writings include YA fantasy as well as short stories. Since completing Remeon's Quest-Earth Year 1930, the prequel in her YA fantasy series, Realms of Chaos, she has been hard at work on the next in the series, scheduled to release August 2020. When she's not hanging out with her characters, her favourite activities are reading, running and spending time with family.
Website: www.jwgarrett.com
BHC Press: www.bhcpress.com/Author_JW_Garrett.html

Animal Instinct
by Carole de Monclin

The breeze carries whispers of her presence.

A shapely form, mesmerising eyes, and a transfixing sway. She's temptation personified.

My legs propel me towards the seductress against my will. Sunlight streams through the leaves, lighting her beautiful face. Long limbs gracefully beckon me.

My insides melt in anticipation. I shouldn't, but instinct defeats reason.

Destiny can't be escaped.

Leaning against her back, I fold her in a sweet embrace. She'll bear strong, healthy children. My children.

Intense pleasure mixes with pain as my life dissolves.

My cruel lover bit off my head, and my body, willingly sacrificed, becomes her feast.

Carole de Monclin *travels both the real world and imaginary ones. She's lived in France, Australia, and the USA; visited 25+ countries; and explored Mars, Ceres, and many distant planets. She writes to invite people on a journey. Her stories can be found in The Arcanist, The Deep Space Anthology, and every volume of the Dark Drabbles series.*
Website: CaroledeMonclin.com
Twitter: @CaroledeMonclin

Honeycomb
by Kevin Berg

Abs have to be the toughest part.

Everything else is easier to shape, to strengthen and tone. To mould and transform to my liking. The abdominal muscles though, they require more work, a special sort of attention.

Washboard—*pfft*, that's nothing.

I lift his shirt and the sweaty wax from thousands of hexagonal prismatic cells glisten in the light. A massive honeycomb writhes and leaks and pulses beneath the thrum of bees, always working, packing the hive with honey and pollen, the wriggle of countless larvae.

If he'd have lived through it all, I suppose he might have smiled too.

Kevin Berg is the author of Indifference, Daddy Monster, and Ants in My Blood. His dark fiction can be found at Pulp Metal Magazine, Near to the Knuckle, The Blood Red Experiment, Horror Sleaze Trash, Trembling With Fear, Underbelly Magazine, Stupefying Stories, and Alien Buddha Press, among others. He currently resides in the Land of Smiles.

My Bloody Partner
by Terri A. Arnold

I can honestly say I've never loved her more than I do at this moment. Neither of us ever desired a partner; I prefer to be alone, and she has always struggled with feelings of inadequacy.

Before I met Lana, I thought I was the only one who felt the thrill of the kill, the only one who truly enjoys it.

She doubts the depth of my love for her, the truth is, she has never looked more beautiful; covered in the stranger's blood, her head tilted back in laughter, the knife balanced perfectly in her hand.

She completes me.

Terri A. Arnold is an avid reader turned writer from a small town in Nova Scotia, who has spent her life reading and wishing she was writing. Although she has written a lot in those years, she has only recently begun to submit pieces for publication. With ongoing encouragement from family and writing challenges with friends, Arnold felt the urge to try her hand at publishing.

Best Friend
by Andrew Anderson

You'll have taken your pills, so I know that you'll be asleep when I sneak back into the house which was once ours.

You never changed the locks.

I can hear you snoring from the foot of the stairs.

I tiptoe up, avoiding the creaky steps—it's unlikely to wake you, but I've taken enough risks already. I just want to spend a little more time with the one I love.

I sit on the floor beside your bed, and Ben pads over.

As I scratch his belly, it saddens me how much I've missed this dog—my best friend.

Andrew Anderson is a spare-time writer of microfiction, flash fiction and short stories, from Bathgate, Scotland. His work has been published on FlashFlood and Re:Written, and published in Black Hare Press anthologies.
Twitter: soorploom

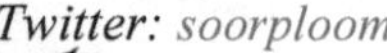

Lip Service
by Clint Foster

Everything in this world is grey now. Everything except for her lips. Red like a flame, like a fiercely beating heart, like the blood in your stool kind of red that shocks you and stabs your eyeballs.

I knew the second I saw those shining red lips, I yearned to have them, I needed them, and even though they do not talk anymore, they kiss just the same. Not quite the same. But I love them just as much as I did the day I took them.

It's not like I was going to let those lips kiss someone else.

Clint Foster lives with his herd of four cats, beloved Basset, Zero, and wonderful wife, Nik. He loves to tell stories just as much as he loves to read them, and is excited to share his work. A longtime consumer of media of all kinds, he enjoys giving back what he hopes everyone else thinks are good stories. Facebook: ClintFosterAuthor

ACKNOWLEDGEMENTS

Huge thanks to all the authors who have contributed to LOVE, the seventh book in the Dark Drabbles series and our fifteenth publication.

We saw a whole new batch of emerging writers submit to this anthology—it was a popular theme—and you all nailed it. So, well done.

We are lucky to be surrounded by great authors who are willing to submit to our anthologies, and we'll continue to showcase their work for as long as they allow us.

As always, a very special *thank you* to you, our loyal and dedicated readers, who continue to support our work.

www.blackharepress.com

Stories of new worlds, new creatures, alien colonisation, humanity's new home, space accidents, alien snackcidents, evil planets, military mashups, alien autopsies, and much, much more.

Beatific angels, holy wars, kitty saviours, epic battles between good and evil, devils and demons, fallen angels and many more tantalising tiny tales.

Wendigos, vampires, things that go bump in the night or hide under the bed, witches, demons, upirs, kelpies, toad people, zombies, sirens and hundreds of other tiny terrifying tales.

Micro myths of the paranormal; poltergeists, spirit boards, ghosts and ghouls, avenging apparitions and horrifying hauntings.

Murder mysteries, criminal chronicles, whodunnits, revenge, suspicion, mayhem, intrigue, and lots more.

A post-apocalyptic adventure of tiny proportions. Venture into the unknown, into a time when society has broken down and every man, woman and child (and the odd monster or alien) must fight for themselves.

Twisted tales of love in tiny portions.

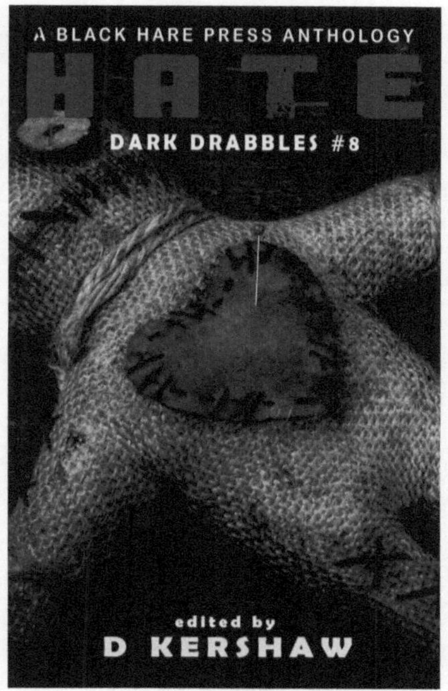

Dark tales of hate and revenge, in bite-sized chunks.

www.ingramcontent.com/pod-product-compliance
Lightning Source LLC
Chambersburg PA
CBHW061043190726
48286CB00006B/1581

9781925809534